Salvation

Fallen Angel series, Book One

By Renee Pace

Salvation

Fallen Angel, Volume 1

Renee Pace

Published by Renee Pace, 2018.

While every precaution has been taken in the preparation of this book, the publisher assumes no responsibility for errors or omissions, or for damages resulting from the use of the information contained herein.

SALVATION

First edition. October 21, 2018.

ISBN: 978-1928178156

Written by Renee Pace.

DEDICATION

TO MY HUSBAND, BRIAN and to my own soul child, Talia. You are my angel and make me have faith. Your three brothers will have their own story as it was foretold.

PROLOGUE

"YOUR ACTIONS HAVE CAST a black mark on your name. You were warned to stay out of this fight. For your disobedience and because you recruited your fellow Cherub sisters to join your independent movement, you will all be punished as an example. Disobeying heavenly decree, no matter what the motivation, is not accepted."

Raphael spoke in *pleb*, the language of the lowest caste, further condemning Isabella by treating her like a commoner. His authoritative voice peppered through the pain gripping her body. She gagged on the blood in her throat. She knew he made his task showy when his pointed whip sliced through the air to punctuate the ending of each sentence, cutting into her already sore and scar-covered back, ensuring she got the message.

Biting the insides of her cheeks, she tasted her own life essence.

"We want to help. We can aid in this heavenly war. We are only striving to serve the greater good." She ground out the words—a feeble attempt to reclaim a semblance of dignity—willing him and the *Septuagint Council*—the thirteen-member council that had ruled against them—to understand their desire for service.

The demons pounding on the heavenly gates were increasing in number, and their attacks into the heavenly realm had only grown more brazen over the years. To sit on the side and watch her brethren fall had been too much for Isabella. A gasp from one of her sisters forced her mind to the present. She almost wished she hadn't.

"Order must be maintained."

Raphael swept out his arm, making Isabella's eyes follow his movement. The black whip reminded her of a coiled snake slithering along behind him to exact her punishment. Standing clustered together, six of the seven Cherub angels, all *novices* like herself, faced the *Septuagint Council.*

"Leave them. This is my crime." Isabella's fear for her sisters caused her courage to slip. Guilt that she had been the one to set this drama into motion weighed heavily on her. She didn't bother speaking in the formal tongue of *scripture,* and went straight to *pleb.* A transgression, adding to her list of Cherub faults that made her different in the eyes of the Council. Her voice, steady, pleased her. Everything else about what had happened to her and her fellow Cherubs who had followed her movement of independence left bile in her throat. *I beg of thee spare them.*

"Judgement has been written. Disobeying Cherub law merits penance. Disobeying the Mistress, who sits on the right hand of the Almighty, merits exile."

Isabella caught the holy glow from the polished *Kita*—the sword ordained to extract punishment. Cold sweat broke out everywhere, and her eyes widened as she choked on the acrid taste of fear, knowing it showed plainly on her face.

Raphael pulled her right wing hard, making it taut.

"Exile! I will take exile!" Her screaming plea met deaf ears.

Raphael moved the sword in a fast arc. Isabella caught the reflected horror mirrored on her sisters' faces. The sword had only been used one other time. Isabella did not want to be the second.

"It is too late for thee Isabella. Thy Mistress did grant thee a small reprieve as she will grant you an audience. Bow thy head to acknowledge thanks."

Swiftly Isabella did, not that her body was capable of much else. She had been ceremoniously draped in the starchy white robe Cherubs wore while undergoing penance but that robe was now shredded from the whip. Her shoulders hunched, and for once Isabella kept her head and eyes downcast, befitting her virginal status when brought before the powerful Council that ruled all the heavenly angels.

Isabella didn't see the *Kita* arch down to sever her wing. Instead she instantly felt the hot loss of her appendage as the nerve roots were brutally hacked through. Searing soul-pain soared like a high off-pitched note through her body. Frozen with the lash of excruciating awareness, she crumpled forward, falling with her arms outstretched as her back bent demonically upward, attempting to escape what came next. Raphael grasped her by the neck, forcing her head down with the sole of his foot, laced in leather-gladiator sandals, to anchor her shuddering body firmly in place.

Isabella screamed until her voice no longer worked. *I have been thrown into the pits of Hell.*

Golden rivers of her life essence, *her blood*, oozed around her shaking body. The sticky substance smelled of dewy blooming flowers, and the liquid instantly soaked itself into her gown.

When each of Isabella's sisters forcibly knelt next to her, Isabella felt her heartbeat triple. She never expected this. A reprimand, yes. But this, it was too much. This was all her fault. Her obsession with the Almighty's children had caused her fall. Her fascination with their culture, their women's independence and sense of freewill had been a seed fermenting in her, creating a longing for more than a Cherub life. Worse, she had led a crusade to entice her fellow sisters to join her in arms when the consequences had been clearly outlined. A Cherub's duty is one of service to a Seraphim and nothing more. It had been the *nothing more* that angered Isabella. Knowing they would all pay the price for her desire for freedom sat like a firey cross in her heart.

The shocked gasps of her sisters stoked that fire and Isabella prayed with her heavenly heart for their forgiveness one day. *They do not deserve this. One day I will make this right.*

That conviction enabled her to endure what came next.

Forcing her head up, she leveled a steady gaze at the Mistress, also known as Mother. Cold and hot, her emotions were as volatile as her moods. The Mistress' neck straightened and for a second Isabella let herself hope she would relent in the punishment.

The Mistress, veiled in a royal dark purple robe that notched at the wrists, wore black gloves to cover her hands, and a barely-visible mesh-like mask covered her face. Not one speck of flesh was visible.

Isabella took the chance. "I accept the punishment, penance and plead with my heavenly heart, Mistress, for you to accept my pain and suffering and not to punish my Cherub sisters." The level of pain racking through Isabella slurred her carefully chosen words. She prayed for the Mistress' compassion.

The Mistress moved closer to Isabella. Overpowered with the sweet scent of rose incense billowing through the somber Council, Isabella did not flinch. A heavy gold circle hung loosely around the Mistress' neck. Another, smaller, necklace with an onyx-colored circle hung even closer to her heart, the black circle a not-so-subtle reminder of the first fallen angel. Its dark color gleamed at Isabella. She wondered if the Mistress would have to wear seven new circles.

"My child, what penance do thee willingly sacrifice for thy fellow sisters?"

Everything in heaven is about sacrifices.

With her life essence no longer streaming from the stubs of her wings, a traitorous thought roared through her mind. *Isn't this enough?* It wasn't of course.

"Spare them and I will grant you anything you ask." Isabella's shaky, pain-filled voice didn't sound like her own. Then again her body was actively protesting the loss of her heavenly wings, which she had cherished. Part and parcel for why they'd been severed from her. Pride. Disobedience. Identity. Traits not warranted in a Cherub.

"This is a lesson thou must learn the hard way, my child. Thy sacrifice is duly noted and that pleases The Almighty greatly. Thy fellow sisters I bless whole, but thou wilt all be exiled to earth."

Hushed but frantic gasps of fear caught at Isabella. She didn't dare dart a look at her Cherub sisters. Exiled to earth, kicked out of the heavens; the harshest of penalties had been passed onto them.

Isabella had not cried when they whipped her. She had not shed a tear when her wings had been sliced off, but she cried now. "I beg thee..."

The Mistress turned back toward the Council. Isabella could have sworn she heard her say, "For the greater good, Isabella, thy will be done."

Chapter One

THE REEK OF ROTTING food filled his senses. Rancid juice seeped through his penance gown making his butt wet and cold. The flimsy material did little to warm him or keep him clean. His first impression of the earthly realm—*disgusting!*

Nathanael stood, automatically arching his wings to take more of his weight as he balanced precariously on the large garbage bags littering the smelly dumpster. Grimacing he stumbled forward, falling fast and hard to the asphalt. He'd forgotten his wings had been removed.

His knees skidded on the hard pavement while his mind balked at the stench, and the unholy sight mankind had created on the Almighty's blessed earth. Blood oozed a golden hue from his ripped knees. While the alley was dark, his angel eyesight enabled him to see clearly. He shivered. *Too bad I can't regulate my body temperature. Earth is cold.*

Standing, he braced his legs apart, automatically moving into his warrior-training mode. *What was I thinking?* A gust of wind brought a pungent fecal odor straight to his nose and he remembered what he'd been thinking. Make right the wrong to his intended mate so he could succeed. Simple, he'd boasted to his brethren, but as he stood on the hard ground of earth he wondered if that would be the case.

Deep in thought, Nathanael didn't hear the men moving from the shadows of the alley until harsh hands pushed him down, grinding his nose and face into the oily slime from the nearby dumpster.

By the blessed blade, I am a fool. Not only a fool, but now I'm covered in grime. Nathanael swore he heard his brethren laughing their collective asses off at him. That, more than being held down, angered him. Nathanael bucked back at his assailants. Shocked when he couldn't dislodge their arms he struggled more, twisting his body this way and that, seeking an opportunity to slip an arm free of their pin-hold. Once free he planned revenge. Plus, they were wasting his precious time. He no more wanted to be on earth than be held down. Humans and heaven-born angels did not mix. Nathanael felt certain that creed was written down in one of the holy books held in the heavenly library.

He was *Sere*, used to fighting but without the support of his wings, his body did not bend the way it should. Muffling a mouth full of obscenities which would have shocked his brethren, he bucked up again, forcing one man to let go.

"Looking for an easy target, are we gentlemen?"

The lyrical voice stole through his brain, gut and heart like a holy light. The woman's words, soft in melody, boomed like liberating bells through his body. And he knew that heavenly voice must belong to the purest of angels, a Cherub. *What is she doing here?* Nathanael twisted his bloodied face, still pinned to the asphalt, until he could see the angel.

One man let go of him to swagger toward a young looking woman. She stood her ground, wearing a costume that made her look anything but Cherub. High-heeled white leather boots encased her calves, leather pants and an ivory-colored top ended above her bellybutton to expose her flesh. Stunned, Nathanael could barely breathe. Cherubs, beautiful in their traditional modest robes, did not hold a candle to this alluring teen taunting the men with her voice and body.

Her leather jacket billowed around her. She gracefully bowed, extending her long torso toward the man. The twinkle of her star-studded belly caught Nathanael's eye, quickening his heart. She made her movements slow, appearing to welcome the man's advance. She tossed her candlelight colored hair over her shoulder as she pivoted one foot behind balancing in a warrior's stance. Nathanael saw a throwing star gleam in her right hand and admiration rose through him. This Cherub could wield her voice to make the man do anything she wanted. Instead, she planned to teach him a lesson in humility.

Contorting his own body, Nathanael slid free of the other man's hold. Without giving his opponent time to jump him again, he leveled a kick to the man's mid-section, noting at the last second the man's eyes were an eerie, unholy green color.

The woman didn't spare him a second glance. "Get back from him. I will take care of this."

Nathanael laughed. "I don't think so."

"And that's your problem." Disdain dripped from her prayer-perfect mouth.

With the glow from the street light he made out a flirt of a smile as it sailed ever so briefly across her lips. Then she let loose her weapon. The six-pointed polished gold throwing star spun and sunk into the man approaching her with ease.

"Just stay out of my way. You are only going to get hurt more, *Sere.*"

Swifter than he anticipated she doused the fallen man's body. The man screamed, his human form dissolved into an oozy green gob of mess on the asphalt, making the alley stink of sulphur, telling Nathanael the woman had used holy water. The realization the human had been demon-turned drew him up sharply.

She somersaulted past him, the click of her heels the only warning, in the small alley as she used her momentum to go after the other man. Nathanael barely scooted out of her way. Another throwing star impacted the man's large chest. Landing on both feet she doused him with another vial of holy water while he sputtered in surprise. Nathanael knew how he felt. Women where he came from did not kill. The demon burst apart, air vaporizing into green puffs of sulphuric mist before falling to the ground. Nathanael watched in awe as she stuck her hand in the green muck to retrieve her weapon. Then she wiped it down and put it back somewhere on the back of her belt.

She then bowed her head to recite an ancient Hebrew prayer of forgiveness, forcing the green muck to further dissolve.

Nathanael carefully eased his way up to her. "Wow, and I thought I did fast prayer."

She ignored him.

Wiping her hands on her pants, she moved to the other puddle of green slime.

"So, Cherub, to whom do I owe the pleasure of thanking?"

She turned and looked at him. For a second something potent filled the space, which considering the reek of garbage milling around them, was miraculous.

"I am no one, *Sere*. But if I were you I'd get some pants on before I leave this alley." A real smile radiating laughter filled her young face. It had to be the loveliest sight Nathanael had ever witnessed.

Nathanael vehemently disagreed with her assessment of being no one.

"And, if I were you *Sere*, I'd fly home." Mockery and contempt met him square on.

He moved a tad closer, noting how her eyes cased him with suppressed laughter but also reading her body language. She was like a lamb, getting ready to bolt. He cursed when she did.

One second there. Another gone.

Nathanael blinked. He had hoped to talk to the Cherub.

"Guess I'll be doing this the old fashion way," he said to himself, moving from the shadows of the alley.

A swirl of thick emotions surged through him. He had been saved by a Cherub angel. A teenager like himself. Glad none of his brothers had witnessed his ass being saved by a mere female, he gathered his composure, and reminded himself he was a Seraphim. Fallen, but angelic, so to speak.

Forced back to the dumpster he dug around until he found a worn sweater. He tugged the filthy thing over his head to cover up his robe and prayed the Seraphim safe house still existed. After the fall of Lucifer, the Council had created angel safe houses ruled and governed by humans wishing to serve the greater good of the Almighty. A few houses over the years had become extinct but Boston was said to still have one. Nathanael could not fail. He had made his choice when he'd begged for exile and now had to complete his task.

TWO NIGHTS LATER NATHANAEL felt more in control of his body and surroundings. He was armed with two small knives braced under his long-sleeved shirt and a third one tucked into his sock. They weren't perfect. But here you worked with what you had. Adaptation, his new word of the day.

He sauntered down the worn, crumbling steps at the back of the recreational center and caught the stench of hashish from a group of teens lingering by the side. They were careful to keep to the shadows as they enjoyed their illegal drugs of the night. Ignoring them, Nathanael opened the door and stepped inside. The symmetry of the place was like any other recreational center but there similarities ended. Since he'd already been to about four such places in the city while searching for his mate, this place with its bar-like décor and freshly painted walls gave him a measure of hope.

Two older teens, with weight lifting bodies, all bulk and muscle with bull dog like necks moved forward.

"These are the rules. No drugs or alcohol on the premises or we'll kick your ass out. And no fighting. Understand?'

Okay, he hadn't expected that and it was on the tip of his tongue to point out a group of druggies were practically camping on the door-step, instead he nodded and mumbled, "Got it."

They let him pass. He made his way through the throng of teens at the center. The symphony of male colognes and female perfumes was overwhelming. *How did humans handle it?* Maneuvering his way through a crowd of thrashing dancers, oblivious to the techno-beat and more in-tune with the light show, he made his way to what looked like a bar. There was mahogany wood for the counter and a dozen bottles in varying shades of copper, red, yellow, lime green and red liquids, all neatly lined up on the backboard.

A large pink neon sign neatly placed between the middle of the bottles stated, "Virgin drinks rule!"

It also looked like someone had at one time scrawled the word, "sucks" underneath the blinking sign. Nathanael chuckled to himself. It was a prank he and his brethren would have probably done and knowing that made him a bit more at ease.

So far this recreational center, located one block up from the Boston Harbor next to a stack of old rundown warehouses, showed promise. He'd learned at the safe house that rumor had it a group of fallen angels were literally singing for their supper. At first he'd dismissed it, thinking his mate would never dare such a thing, but with little else to guide him, he'd been force to pursue the wild tale, all the while praying with his divine heart he'd be wrong.

The stabbing colors from the light show hurt his sensitive eyes. So much color. So much of everything. Again the thought he was out of his element overwhelmed him. He chose his path. He'd fight for his Cherub angel and make her come back with him. After spending only forty-eight hours on earth, Nathanael couldn't wait to get back to the pristine, orderly world of angels, where everything was preordained from birth. Status meant everything. You were born by the grace of The Almighty to be a certain type of angel and Nathanael knew he'd been born to be a warrior, all the way.

No Cherub will stand in my path. I will ascend. Or die trying.

"Can I help you?" A man, who looked in his late twenties, and who stood behind the bar wearing a dark navy suit nailed him with a stony look. The man, all business, appraised Nathanael's attire. Donning the normal teenage clothing of the decade had been a necessity but the tight jeans made him conscious he was overly tall compared to most youths and much more muscular. The black dress jacket over his long-sleeved shirt he'd purchased on a whim after going to the Seraphim safe house. What he had discovered there didn't sit well with him.

None of the earth-bound angels wanted anything to do with the heavenly exiled Cherubs. They knew of their existence but didn't interact with them and that confused Nathanael.

Why would they treat them with scorn? They were females and if Nathanael had his way they would be protected by the earth-born Seraphim. When he had mentioned that the Patriarch of the house had silenced him. Nathanael had wanted to argue his point but the Patriarch had made it clear they had approached the fallen angels and been told to leave them alone. Why the man listened to them mystified Nathanael. The fallen angels needed protecting and while he had pleaded his case late into the night, the Patriarch would not budge. If the female angels needed him they had to come to the Seraphim safe house and not the other way around. Frustrated, Nathanael had left. He felt more disgusted with his brethren than anything else. A Seraphim was a warrior, but it would appear on earth the earth-born angels were made up mostly of lawyers, bankers and business men.

Scanning the crowd, Nathanael vowed tonight to discover where his Cherub was and return with her to the heavenly realm for good. Then in a decade's time they'd undergo the *x'simcha* ceremony, binding two souls together to breed future Seraphim if they were boys and future Cherubs if they were girls. Simple. They way of heaven-born angels.

"Take it you understand the rules here," stated the man, who still eyed him suspiciously.

Nathanael nodded.

"And this is your first time in the area?"

Nathanael knew the man was fishing for information, but the last thing he wanted was conversation with another useless human. "What do you recommend for a drink?" he asked changing the subject.

The man gave a crafty smile like he knew he'd been purposely mislead and said, "Scorched Earth."

"What?" asked Nathanael.

"The drink Scorched Earth is what I'd recommend for you."

Nathanael nodded and the guy handed him a blood-colored drink, a mix of some of the copper liquid, some from the red and some from a bottle the bartender had under the counter. The drink cost Nathanael six dollars. Nathanael paid for his beverage, smiled and leaned back against the counter, taking a sip of the syrupy drink. Bitterness singed his throat and he coughed up a storm.

The man chuckled as he went on to serve another customer. Nathanael was not one bit amused. Whatever was in the drink tickled his throat, but once he calmed down the warmth from the bitter liquid enveloping his belly wasn't all that unpleasant.

The bartender rematerialized by Nathanael "So, what brings you to these parts?"

The question was straight up asking what Nathanael was doing here. It was also a not so subtle warning this human didn't trust him.

"I'm looking for someone."

"There's lots of someone's here. Anyone in particular? I know most of the regular teens and some of the ones no longer allowed in here."

"Are you the manager?" asked Nathanael, trying to get a sense if the human really could be helpful.

The human chuckled. "I guess you could call me that. Most days I feel like I'm the janitor, guidance counselor, and accountant all rolled into one. This building is mine. This rec center is also mine so if you're looking for trouble take it elsewhere. I've spent a lot of money on this place trying to make it inviting for the teens in this area."

"Certainly looks better than the last one I was in. All they had were rows of tables and the kids were bored to tears playing some stupid game called Bingo," said Nathanael, taking a second tentative sip of the brew.

"That would be Caldwell's Recreational Center. The city owns that hell hole and it's totally useless. Listen, I've got to chat with someone back stage but if you need another drink or want to talk later I'll be back."

Nathanael smiled and nodded. *Maybe the human wasn't all that bad.*

Quiet transcended the bar the minute the shimmering lights and techno beat ceased. A hush of anticipation soared through the motley teenagers.

Caught up in the anticipation, Nathanael felt his body gravitate toward the stage. A mass of excited people, four levels deep, stood between him and the dark backdrop. Muffled conversations and hushed whispers thickened the air. The mood in the place moved from partying delight to sweet ecstasy. The curtains swung up like a billowing cloud and there before him stood four Cherubs, their heavenly bodies on display in clothing that would make the Mistress weep. Each wore a pleated black and white skirt barely covering their bottoms, high top red sneakers with black laces that travelled all the way up to the knees and white blouses tied into halter tops which showcased more of their honey-colored heavenly flesh.

You are kidding me. Nathanael blinked. For a moment he wondered if this fantasy come true was real, especially since he hadn't stopped thinking about the sexy Cherub from the alley. Shifting on his feet to ease his discomfort, he moved closer to the stage.

Two members of the band had blonde hair that fell in tight ringlets to their waist, one had straight pixie-cropped white hair with red dyed ends framing her small face, but the one center stage bore the traditional thick straight blonde locks of a Cherub, and she was the female who had saved him in the alley. A tiny gold star embedded in her belly-button winked at him. Her skin tone glowed like a warm candle and she, like the rest of the Cherubs, looked about seventeen. With the thick outline of black make-up around their eyes they were a spell-binding sight.

So these were the teens who had dared to take up arms and lead the heavenly charge against the demons pounding on Heaven's gates. Knowing that speed up his heart more because without a doubt these Cherubs were like none he'd ever seen or envisioned.

The hush in the center grew. Nathanael became acutely aware of his own ragged breathing. Nathanael eyed the lead Cherub. She wasn't wearing anything remotely angelic. His heart leapt, eager for the sound of her heavenly voice.

A bell rang, a second and third. A soft, haunting melody of a hum started, growing louder with each Cherub until the girl at center stage, threw her head back and sang. The wail of the sorrow-filled song crashed through every fiber of his being, but the seductive tenor also teased the audience.

There, standing at center stage, was the Cherub who had rescued him two days ago. Then she had taken on the demon-infested humans with deadly throwing stars. Tonight she stroked each person's soul, allowing the purity of her voice to work its magic, easing their anxiety, allowing them in this moment to let their heart truly love, and feel the power of her heavenly lyrics. The sexy sound traveled through Nathanael's bones.

Every cell in Nathanael's Seraphim body recognized the sensual lilt and the foreign words she sung. Ancient Hebrew, the cadence rolled off her tongue like the taste of heavenly red wine. She flirted with the crowd, who were oblivious to the sexual meaning of her words. Her words caused the fine hairs on his skin to rise with pleasure. If he'd had his wings they'd be arched back, proudly displayed. Shaking his head, Nathanael forced his body to cool, taking another dreaded sip of his drink, wanting the bitter tang, anything to force his mind to heel from the fantasy he was envisioning. When the remaining Cherubs threw their voices into the melody of the song, a flood of such intense love slammed into him, he felt like he'd had one too many *urdal*—the blessed seeds from the heavenly plant many Seraphim chewed to experience a more divine holy prayer.

Nathanael worked his way through the crowd. A few people he shouldered out of the way until he was close enough to the right of the stage to lean against the wall and watch. A total of four more songs followed.

By the end of their first set his breathing was labored, his heart pounded loudly in his chest and his palms were sweaty.

He moved from the wall to flex his muscles. A part of him was angry. However, he wasn't sure if that emotion was directed at himself or the teens on stage.

What he'd witnessed felt sacrilegious and it burned through him. Glad he'd taken on the mission to extract his future heavenly wife he prayed that tonight he'd be back in heaven's realm. The minute he found her, he'd call to the Mistress and as promised she'd let them back into the heavenly realm, once his Cherub to be wife agreed to the wedding. Then he'd repent for the impurity of his thoughts. Again he shifted, wishing his jeans weren't so tight as he tried to calm his emotions.

He prayed one of these Cherubs wasn't Isabella. He didn't want her to be openly displaying her body or voice for mankind. Cherub angels were purity. They exemplified all the heavenly descriptions of what that word entailed.

Marching toward the back of the stage, he wondered why no one stopped him. Cherub angels were never unescorted in the heavens yet here on earth they walked about alone, vulnerable.

A sharp steel blade cut into his throat, catching him off guard.

"Well, what do we have here? Why I do believe it's a Seraphim and just my luck, the one I saved from the alley the other night. To whom do we owe the pleasure of addressing?"

The feel of his own angelic blood sliding down his throat caused Nathanael to attempt to move back. The blade cut more into his flesh, making it painfully obvious the Cherub with the sharp knife wouldn't think twice about ending his existence. Casting aside his anger and stupidity, he recognized he was intrigued by these Cherub teens with their macho-*Sera* attitudes.

"I am Nathanael, First Born of the House of Raphael."

A gasp stole through the other three angels but not the one controlling the knife.

"Why, *Sere,* are you here on earth?"

Contempt and hatred spilled from the voice, which only moments before had had him almost on his knees, heart fluttering wildly in reverence. The knife was held expertly in the hand of the band's lead singer.

"I am here to find Isabella and bring her home," he said.

"Why?" the leader asked.

"She is to be my future heavenly wife and I have come to claim her."

"Like hell," she said, twisting around to confront him face to face.

Demon daggers looked more inviting than the leader's pale blue eyes as they narrowed in hatred. Her jaw clenched shut so hard he heard the click of her teeth, as her knife cut deeper into his throat causing more of his golden-hued life essence to flow down his throat onto his collar.

Chapter Two

"IZZY!" MEREDITH'S EXCLAMATION cut through the taut-wire tension.

Isabella sliced her Cherub sister and best friend a silencing look.

"I think it best if you remove your knife, sister."

The reprimand came from Shea, the only Cherub in the group who still attended daily worship four times a day. Shea's hair, like Izzy's still the traditional length, fell in curly waves to her waist. Shea, who had to be forced to wear the on-stage costume, tended to follow proper decorum, praying for the day the Heavenly Gates once again accepted them. It wasn't in Izzy to tell her again and again those gates had been sealed shut from the likes of them.

Now this Seraphim angel with his broad quarterback shoulders, six-foot-six height, thick muscled thighs, chiseled square jaw and stormy gray eyes had invaded their homemade haven. Anger rooted itself like a fast growing vine, twisting in her gut. *This must be part of my penance.* The Seraphim looked to be a little older than her seventeen years. She judged him to be about nineteen. Too bad she hadn't aged a day since being cursed from the heavens. None of them had aged and not one of them liked that part of the punishment. Charcoal-colored hair cut to human military precision marked him a *Sere*, a step below becoming a full-fledged *Sera* warrior. Then he'd let his hair grow to the traditional shoulder length. To become *Sera* he must first find his *b'iā*, preordained by the Mistress, of course.

That is the reason he is here. Not to rescue me or us, but so he can become a true angel warrior. We don't really matter to him. I am just a means for his advancement.

"I take it you are Isabella."

His soft but rough voice reminded her of dry timber. One spark and that quiet voice could roar to life. Knowing that, she wisely followed Shea's advice and withdrew her knife. Tucking it back inside the bodice of her gown, his eyes followed her hand. She cut him a crafty look.

Izzy didn't say anything. Instead she waited for him to press.

"You are also the Cherub from the alley." It wasn't a question and she noted how he avoided stating the obvious. She had saved his ass.

Her latest outburst of blasphemy elicited another Hebrew word inked in the traditional semi-cursive lettering of Rashi script to be burned into her flesh, making her itch. Pleased she hadn't said another swear word out loud while thinking a dozen more in her head, she didn't dare let on to her sisters how much her body ached. Only Meredith knew the true extent of the Mistress' curse.

"Yes, I am the Cherub who killed the demons you had drawn to the area. You are lucky I was on my way home. Otherwise you'd be enjoying the fires of..."

"I had gathered that myself, Izzy."

"Isabella," she corrected. No way did she want her nickname rolling of his tongue.

He nodded. The movement caused his eyes to glide knowingly down her body. Izzy hated her breathless reaction to his bold assessment. She also hated how sinful looking his lips were and how the smell of him, bold male with a hint of exotic spices, reminded her of home.

"Why are you looking at me like that?" she barked. Palms sweaty, she resisted wiping them on her leather pants.

"Wondering where else you might be hiding knives, my *b'iä*."

Isabella got right into his face. Squaring her shoulders back she calmly said, "Never. Do not ever call me that. I am not nor ever will be your...your, oh hell. I will never be your heavenly wife." Izzy gasped, as the fresh burn from the use of the swear word, hell, caused more Rashi script to scorch her right butt cheek. Worse, the way he'd said *b'iā* made her heart soar, the feeling reminding her of flying through warm clouds. Her penance was getting a lot harder.

Stomping away from him, Izzy marched up the stairs to the third floor of the apartment building. Ten years ago, when they got kicked out of the heavens, the seven of them had quickly learned they needed to band together and work toward a common goal. Getting the Mistress to grant them back into the heavenly realm had been their first priority while assimilating into mankind. Now, Izzy's task was to keep her sisters safe and make their lives on earth bearable.

"Why are you not at the Cherub safe house?" asked the Seraphim called Nathanael.

She tried to recall him but couldn't. In fact, born of the house of Raphael, she wondered if he knew it had been his father who had severed her wings. Izzy hadn't thought of her wingless form in years and doing so now elicited a deep ache within her. One she tried at all times not to examine too closely. Her sisters always took care to keep their own wings invisible and that act of kindness while warming her heart, still felt like a slap in the face. She, no matter what, would never be angel again.

"Never fear, Seraphim, we went, but realized fast we were better on our own. After a decade here we have established our own place on earth. *M'sumli sere q'ulat ch'eei* – welcome to our blessed dwelling *Sere.*" Izzy used *scripture,* letting him know she had been taught the traditions of Cherub culture.

"What did you say?" he demanded, commanding the steps like he owned the stairwell.

"If you can't recognize civility, far be it for me to—"

"No, you said a decade. What do you mean?" His voice sounded agitated.

Izzy turned the moment her heel reached the top step of the well-worn wooden stair. When she had enough money she'd add fresh paint to the hall and walls and get her business partner to strip the wood off the stairs. Staring down at him, she took the time to admire his flawless face, instantly reminding her of all that had been in her life.

"We've been here a decade. In case you can't count, Seraphim. That's ten years. Ten years serving our exile. And if you are hard of hearing, Meredith can write it out formally for you."

Izzy turned and dismissed him, enjoying the sound of her clicking heels as she sauntered to her private bedroom. Opening the door with a key she walked through, leaving her sisters to entertain their new guest. She, on the other hand, made straight for the large bathroom. A hot bath with the soothing scents of jasmine oil had her name stamped on them. No way could she look into that Seraphim's eyes one more time. Hearing him call her his *b'iā*, his heavenly host of a wife, had resurrected something foreign and what she had thought long-dead within her—the need to be a dutiful Cherub. Serving the Seraphim would end her penance but steal her away from her sisters. She knew what choosing a *b'iā* meant—preordained destinies tied to one heart, one heavenly soul and Izzy wanted desperately to escape it all.

Izzy couldn't wait to get out of the high top sneakers and pleated skirt and shirt. Her stomach felt slightly nauseous as the erotic visions of unrestricted pleasure, the type she'd been taught since she'd undergone puberty, wormed their way through her subconscious. She had to find a way to get rid of Nathanael soon or risk everything she'd fought for. Independence, free will and a life other than the preordained Cherub one she'd been born into. Life on earth wasn't anything like living in the heavenly realm but at least here Izzy got to think for herself. Ascending again didn't matter to her. Or so she told herself.

Damn! The Mistress sent Nathanael knowing he offered salvation— the way to serve her penance, accordingly. Honor her Cherub teachings and culture, and allow this Seraphim to breed with her. That might delight her teachers but Izzy thought, *not in my lifetime.* Tempted to curse her frustration aloud, she decided a cooler head was warranted. Turning on the cold water she ran her head under the stream until the ice cold shocked her; a brutal but necessary reminder. While the pleasure of a hot bath might be desirable, in the heavenly realm, sacrifices rule.

Chapter Three

NATHANAEL WATCHED ISABELLA leave. She was the leader of this group of Cherubs and knowing she was also the same teen who rescued him left him feeling unmanned. It wasn't a feeling he liked. He watched as the cluster of other girls spoke amongst themselves, but none went after Isabella. In this realm she was the ruler and her unspoken desire for privacy overrode their curiosity.

"Where has she gone?" asked Nathanael to the Cherub who had forced Isabella to remove the knife from his throat.

The Cherub immediately looked down at the floor, keeping her eyes downcast as was the norm and quietly spoke. Nathanael had to strain his hearing and move slightly forward to hear her words over the pounding sounds of the DJ's music.

"We are honored you have found us, Nathanael. I am Meredith."

Nathanael waited a heartbeat for her to continue with the full litany of her formal name, but none came forward. It dawned on him then what the true meaning of their exile meant. They had given up their family names as a sign of respect to not disgrace their heavenly sisters.

"Isabella needs some time to adjust, Nathanael. Things on Earth have not been easy."

Nathanael wanted specifics but at that moment the other Cherubs moved closer and he immediately noticed how Meredith clenched her jaw and tensed. He got the distinct impression she would not say anything more about their exile while the other Cherubs were present.

"Take me to her," he demanded, wanting and needing answers now.

Meredith moved slightly out of reach. "Certainly, but..."

He waited, raising his eyebrow as the time stretched on.

She ushered her sisters over forcing Nathanael to wait. It wasn't a feeling he liked.

"Sisters let us retire to our residence to refresh our souls," said Meredith, gently coaxing the other Cherubs to lead the way from back stage to their dwelling.

Nathanael wisely kept his mouth shut as he followed them out the backstage exit door. A covered walkway led to another building. This building, all dark brown brick, blended in more with the night. The building looked in better shape than the center sitting in front of it, obscuring its view of the run down block. Meredith was the one who held open the door for him allowing him to enter their quarters. Nathanael noticed how quiet the Cherubs all moved as they ascended the stairs to a top loft. There they split off, but Meredith was the one who urged him into what looked like a common area. Large waist high windows framed the front of the building. Nathanael noticed the pristine cleanliness of the place and how white everything was, including the leather sofas and walls. He moved to the window and was amazed at how even two flights up the scenery changed. He'd been wrong. They had a wonderful eagle-eyed view of the Boston harbor and he highly suspected the amount of light streaming through the high windows in the day would make the room almost holy like.

Turning he faced Meredith. Very briefly their eyes made contact, but swiftly like she'd been raised she bowed her head and waited for him to speak.

"Where is she?"

"Isabella has gone through a lot, Nathanael," said Meredith.

That was twice she'd warned him about his mate and his gut told him her words weren't meant to protect him rather warn him. "What happened to you all?" asked Nathanael.

"Exile to Earth is not for the faint of heart and we've been here so long..."

It cut through him again, what Isabella had said. A decade. These angels, teens who should be cloistered away until their intended came for them, had somehow managed to survive in amongst the filth of mankind for ten long years. A part of him yearned to ask how, but he didn't want Meredith to be the one to explain things to him and he highly suspected she wouldn't even if he exerted his Seraphim right.

"Meredith in the Heavens you have only been gone a week."

Her gasp and faint pallor of skin forced him into action. He urged her down toward the sofa, careful to not touch her.

"You must be wrong."

Nathanael shook his head. "No. I am not. I cannot believe the Mistress left you alone for so long."

Meredith closed her eyes. "Without Isabella, your intended, we would have perished into the sins of man. She saved us. You must go to her and tell her what you have disclosed to me. Make her see reason for us to continue with prayer to the Mistress. Surely you are a sign we are back in her blessings."

Nathanael wasn't so certain that was the case. It had taken him days and lots of begging to convince the Mistress to grant him exile to Earth to search for his mate, but that didn't explain why the Cherubs had stopped praying and paying their respects to the Mistress. It went against their nature. Surely he heard wrong.

"Isabella will want nothing to do with you, Nathanael but you must gain her trust if we are ever to have hope of ending our penance," said Meredith, looking more like herself, composed. "Her sanctuary is on the top floor, the door at the end of the hall."

Nathanael nodded and made his way to the one Cherub who was his even though he highly suspected she was going to fight him all the way.

"You think to avoid this discussion."

The nerve of him. Nathanael sat on the white duvet of her bed, a stark imposing figure. It felt like a slap in the face. After all she'd gone through she tried not ever to think of home. Now, him sitting there like he owned the place when it had been her sweat and voice that bought the brownstone, infuriated her. He had no right to make himself at home in her sanctuary. Izzy's eyes darted everywhere trying in vain to ignore the sight of his naked feet. Following tradition, he'd placed his black leather shoes next to the door of her bedroom. By the blessed scribes that unnerved her.

Towel draped tightly around her body, Izzy fought not to shiver. "Get out!"

"I don't think so." His bold statement snapped her cool reserve.

"How dare you? How dare you come now? Why?"

He rose, moving into her space. She didn't budge. The heavenly scent of his Seraphim body streamed through her senses. He smelled decadent, forbidden, a hint of masculine sweat telling her he wasn't immune to her or the intimate setting. Everything about him had been made to match her, including the height of his tall frame and deep voice. He might look like a teenager on the cusp of adulthood, but she highly suspected he was well versed in all aspects of Seraphim culture, including mating. That notion caused her eyes to narrow in annoyance.

That's the problem with Cherub culture. Everything works to his advantage.

A breath away from her, he stared openly at her now shivering form. "You are going to catch a cold. You are being irrational. I will wait outside for you to dress and then we will discuss all of this, civilly and in the proper way of things."

He didn't wait for her assent. Why should he? He was Seraphim. He commanded and she was to obey. Loudly, Izzy huffed. *Dream on!*

A list of blasphemous words almost spewed off her tongue. Not wishing her entire body to be inked in Rashi scrip, Izzy bit her tongue and watched with pleasure when he strolled out of her bedroom. Turning her task to finding more appropriate clothing, she quickly yanked on her skinny jeans and a tight t-shirt. She pulled on her black hoodie as Gareth opened her window to slide into her room.

His stealth alarmed her. Any other person would be dead. Technically, Nathanael wasn't human so the fact he'd dared to enter her sanctuary was partly acceptable. Gareth, on the other hand, knew her boundaries.

He grinned. The emerald-green of his eyes sparkled with mischief. By the path of light, he disarmed her and for a human male that was not a good thing.

"Surprised?"

"That's an understatement. Why are you here, Gareth?" asked Izzy.

The door burst open, a blur of bulky speed moved through and the next thing Izzy heard was a crash as Nathanael grasped Gareth and wrestled him to the floor. The dark gleam in Nathanael's gray eyes as he rushed into her room looked deadly and in that one condemning glance he reminded Izzy of his father, Raphael, the angel who had severed her wings. Feeling dizzy with the onslaught of that most painful, most humiliating memory, it took her a moment to realize Nathanael meant business. He pushed his knife deeper into Gareth's neck. In their heavenly realm, if a male entered a Cherub's sanctuary who wasn't her soul-mate, a quick death followed.

"Get off him!" Izzy made her feet move toward them.

Gareth had the good sense not to move a muscle, but his angry look warned he sought blood. It was a look she had never witnessed on his boyishly charming face and after two years of intense friendship she thought she'd seen all sides of him. She'd been wrong.

Nathanael gave her a cold look. "You know this..."

She knew he struggled not to say *human* with the disgust and contempt a Seraphim felt. Ten years ago when she'd fallen to earth, alive, her body in the grips of agonizing pain it had been humans who had tended to her wounds. Tender, caring hands worked their own miracle on her abused body. They'd had no words to aptly describe what they'd discovered on her back. They assumed she'd been mutilated but they were shocked her blood ran yellow. The kindness of those humans who had not asked a lot of questions, but who instead allowed her to heal, Izzy still felt to the marrow of her bones. She'd shrugged off their psychiatrists who had looked for mind scars. What she had suffered could only be described as a soul wound—one that to this day had not healed. Two hard knobs of flesh still protruded from her back. Reminders of her wings. She hadn't let the plastic surgeon come near them, fleeing the moment her body had mended. Humans did not deserve the disparaging angels gave them. They were not all evil and not all had fallen far from *H'uluan*—the Garden of Eden.

"This is Gareth. He is welcome among us." Izzy kept her eyes trained on Nathanael, not daring a look in Gareth's direction. She'd deal with him later. After the knife was removed from his throat.

With deliberate slowness, Nathanael moved the knife off Gareth's throat. Casually he backed off his bulk anchoring Gareth to the wooden floorboards. Gareth leapt to his feet and by the fierce expression on his face, Izzy knew all hell was about to be let loose in her bedroom. She didn't blame Gareth. Nathanael seemed to have that effect. However, as military prepared as Gareth might be, an even match to Nathanael, never. Angels were far superior in strength to humans. Izzy discovered that first hand when she'd encountered her first demon.

"Explain yourself," commanded Nathanael, his voice sounding as low as the vibration of a plucked string from a double-bass.

"Who is he talking to?" asked Gareth. "Cause I know that boy isn't speaking to me. I was behaving, Izzy, but tell wacko to leave."

"Wacko?"

"In case you haven't figured that out buddy, that's you." Gareth moved closer to Izzy, imposing his muscular body between her and Nathanael.

Izzy fought not to smile. "Enough. That's enough from the two of you. I want you both to leave."

"No frigging way, Izzy am I leaving you alone with this pit bull."

"What's a pit bull?" asked Nathanael, trying hard to follow the conversation. She knew how that felt also, but bittersweet memories of assimilating into human culture had to be stored away for another time.

"It's a dog, you moron," clarified Gareth, stepping toward Nathanael, and clenching his fists for show.

"This *human* dares to call me a dog. Isabella, I have had enough. Dismiss this man now. We need to talk. I am no longer inclined to play nice."

Wow, if that was playing nice, she didn't want to see his mean side. "Nathanael, can you give me a few minutes with Gareth, alone?" *Why the hell am I asking his permission?*

"You heard her buddy, sod off and leave us," barked Gareth.

"Cut that out, Gareth, or I'll make you leave too," said Izzy, reprimanding Gareth when she felt he too deserved it.

Nathanael moved toward Izzy and damned if her body didn't sway slightly in his direction. "Five minutes. Then he leaves and we talk." Bold declarations, typical Seraphim.

Nodding, Izzy turned her attention back to folding her clothes she'd removed while looking for her favorite hoodie. She was glad now she'd chosen black. The color certainly fit her mood. The minute Nathanael left she focused on Gareth, catching the slight shake in his hands, hearing his heart do that fast flutter, knowing he fought the good fight because she had asked him. After two years of friendship, him patiently waiting for her, she told him her terms. Get clean, purify your body and then she'd give him hers. It had sounded simple, even reasonable considering she'd thought she'd never see the Heavenly Gates again. Certainly she didn't think for one minute her soul-mate would come looking for her. She couldn't explain to Gareth she loved him like a brother she'd never had. Telling him *that* would crush him, because she knew he longed for her body and heart.

Those two things were no longer hers. They belonged to Nathanael. He was her other half. She hated him all the more for his existence.

"Care to explain who the hell he is?" Gareth plopped down on her bed. It made her uncomfortable and always did. That's why she'd told Meredith to stop letting him sneak into her sanctuary. Guess her friend still wasn't listening to her.

"He's an—"

"Don't you dare tell me he's an old friend. That's bullshit and you know it. Who is he? We share everything. No secrets, right?"

Izzy looked away. Her life for the past decade, based on lies, held more secrets than she dared ever disclose.

Gareth went for the flesh to flesh approach. Before, when he'd touch her she'd told herself feeling nothing was a normal reaction. She might be a fallen Cherub but she was still an angel and he a human. Knowing how her body reacted, heated and bloody well ached with Nathanael's nearness, rubbed her wrong. She wanted her body to feel like that when Gareth touched her. It didn't.

"Izzy, what's wrong?" His note of compassion and tenderness almost opened the floodgate of emotions she had locked and buried away for eternity.

Shaking out of his light embrace, she laughed. "Nothing. He's a member of my family." *That most certainly is true, just not how I really mean it.*

"Like a cousin or something?" questioned Gareth, seeking clarification and allowing her to move further away.

"Or something. It's complicated." *Like on a scale you could not imagine.* "He's visiting for a while but he'll be gone soon." *One can only pray for that.* "Why did you really come here, Gareth? You know I'm uncomfortable with you in my bedroom."

Seeing his large, six-foot-four frame silhouetted against her wall from the moonlight sneaking in from the partially opened window, she'd realized he looked a lot like Nathanael. With his dark military shaved head, defined muscular arms and prize fighter body, he could pass for Seraphim. The arm of black tattoos that bore two names, Eddie and Frank, set him apart. His ink bore the names of his buddies, killed during a tour of duty in Iraq. They were constant reminders his life, like hers, hadn't been all rosy.

That realization shook her. Had she been drawn to him because of that? Hoping it wasn't so, Izzy sat down on the bed, motioning for Gareth to join her.

"Do you want me to sing for you?" She'd do this for him tonight, knowing Nathanael probably had his ear to her door. If he dared intervene she'd throw one of her nearby throwing stars at him. That thought brought a fleeting smile to Izzy's face.

Seeing her warming look, Gareth grasped her hand. She allowed him the dignity to respond in his quiet fashion. Thumb stroking her thumb, he nodded.

Reaching for the purity of her heavenly voice was an easy task. Leashing the swirl of strange emotions Nathanael had unwound, not so much. Like her fellow Cherubs, she'd been taught how to sing since the moment she could stand. She clasped his hand so they were bound prayer-like together and then Izzy started. He liked the old songs, so she sang him an ancient Hebrew ballad watching his body absorb her healing notes. Tension eased from his shoulders, his eyes closed in serenity and his heartbeat slowed. She loved how her voice affected him so.

"Thank you, Izzy. Thanks. I'm feeling better."

"I'm really proud of you, Gareth. You're doing good. You're a strong soldier."

He simply nodded, but she caught the slight well of tears in his eyes. *We all have our demons to fight.* Izzy was glad hers were ones she had the opportunity to vanquish on a regular basis in the flesh, and not tormenting her every waking moment like Gareth's. His demons slept in his mind. The survivor always lives with guilt and that question of 'why me?' No one knew that better than Izzy.

"I needed to come here. I needed you, tonight."

"I know," she soothed.

"You understand?"

"Of course. That's why I'm here for you. It's been a long night, Gareth. It's time you left. I'll see you tomorrow, okay?"

"You promise?" The plea in his voice told her his fight was hard.

"I promise. Tell Meredith if you have need of me. She'll understand." Izzy stood up from the bed and made her way to the door. Gareth followed.

When he leaned down to kiss her goodnight, Izzy stopped him. "Goodnight, Gareth."

Straightening, he said, "Tomorrow, Izzy."

Closing the door softly behind her, Izzy leaned against the wood trying to gather her composure and strength. She felt like she'd been in a battle for days but that wasn't the case. The only war waging within Izzy was in her soul. She'd rather deal with demons. The last person she wanted to confront was Nathanael. When a soft knock sounded she tensed. "Come in."

Meredith walked in carrying a hot cup of herbal tea. "This is for you."

"Thank the blessed light. I thought you were Nathanael."

"No, he left. He said you've had a busy night and thought you might need something to soothe your soul. His words exactly. I had...I had, forgotten..."

"How formal everything is. How unemotional a Seraphim sounds?"

Meredith handed her the hot mug. "Nathanael didn't sound unemotional, Izzy. He sounded concerned. While you were talking with Gareth he asked us some questions. Did you know in heaven only a week has gone by? That's why he sounded surprised when you said ten years. He had no idea. None of the heavenly angels know that time on earth moves differently. We've been pining away on earth thinking they don't care, when they've counted only seven days of our exile. Why?"

Izzy closed her eyes wearily. She highly doubted no heavenly angels knew of their plight. *Why indeed?* Taking a sip of the hot brew, she wondered where Nathanael had gone.

"He's staying at the Seraphim safe house. Oh, he asked me to give you this."

Meredith held out a small white cloth. Unwrapping the offering, Izzy's heart plummeted to her feet. If her wings still existed she'd have them protectively curled around her, enveloping her so that no one, especially her best friend, could see the reaction on her face. There nestled in the center of the white cloth an onyx-colored stone with a small hole at the top, held onto a plain leather tie. The same necklace she had suspected that had been wound around the Mistress' neck.

"Tell him I can't accept." She choked out the words, wrapping the cloth back up to hand it back to Meredith.

"I'll take this for you now, but you must tell him you can't accept. He's coming tomorrow after our show to speak with you. Looks like your angel's here to rescue you."

For the first time Izzy noted the hurt and scorn filling Meredith's usually calm voice. Izzy reached for Meredith's hand, drawing her closer to look into her sad eyes. "Meredith, you can't begin to imagine that I plan to leave."

Meredith gave her one of her famous 'are you nuts' looks. "You are Cherub. He is Seraphim. I distinctly heard his words. You are his heavenly wife. He holds the power to bond you to him, as is the right of a Seraphim."

Izzy took hold of her friend firmly by the shoulders and let her anger and disappoint reign free. "I did not bear arms in the heavenly war to simply become a vessel to carry forth the next generation. I did not willingly sacrifice my wings for this. I will fight this. Like I've fought for everything in my and our lives. I will not leave you. You are all my Cherub sisters and more than that you are my best friend. Without you, all of you, I am nothing."

Meredith leaned in, allowing Izzy to hug her. Both in tears, Izzy finally released her friend, who had suffered like her with the exile. They all had suffered and would continue to, until the Mistress declared they had served their penance. Abandoning them was not an option. She'd rather cut out her heart than sacrifice them to live on earth alone without her. Killing a demon was a hundred times easier than dealing with the onslaught of emotions she'd experienced today and once again Nathanael was at fault.

Why did he have to find us? Find me?

In her heart, Izzy knew the answer. Without her he couldn't ascend. What he wanted condemned her. A Seraphim did not account for her wishes. She was Cherub. A female brought up to please him in all aspects, to never question his authority and to keep his heavenly house pure and serene. Nothing about her at the moment, including Izzy's thoughts, was pure. She'd rather sharpen knives than keep his house clean.

Chapter Four

NAT DIDN'T GO BACK to the Seraphim safe house. His heart felt heavy, his soul ached and his mind had a dozen questions circling over and over again. The intensity of what he'd discovered tonight left him feeling more than dazed. A part of him was questioning all he'd been taught, all he knew. And it was all Isabella's fault. That, he didn't like. He walked to the only place he could think of, a nearby synagogue. Saturday night, the beginnings of holy night. Late into the evening, almost midnight, he thought it empty. Until a door opened and a hand waved him inside.

"Can I help you, son?"

The gruff voice was filled with caring. Nat took the offered invitation, needing to cleanse his emotions. He searched within himself for that steel-honed Seraphim, the mighty warrior he was supposed to become and found himself lacking.

"Thank you." He stepped through the door feeling the wide space of the synagogue stretch before him. His gaze moved lovingly to the large eight-foot high wooden *heichal*, the Torah ark, looking like an exact copy of the one in the Seraphim Prayer house. He blinked, twice, wondering if this was a sign.

"You look like you've lost your best friend, if you don't mind my observation," said the person who obviously was the Rabbi.

"Something like that," mumbled Nat.

Dressed in traditional dark robes wearing what humans called a *kippah*, a small white head covering, the Rabbi looked quite old. His gray beard reached his chest and wrinkles marred his face, making him look kind and thoughtful. Nat didn't understand the dress code, but this wasn't his culture. Seraphim angels most certainly did not cover their heads when praying to the Almighty. Their prayer robes were white, not dark in color and underneath their robes angels wore nothing. Purity of mind and body to help cleanse the soul.

The Rabbi swept him further inside the wide space. The smell of polished pine lingered in the air, and worn leather along with a hint of incense filled him, bringing him a measure of peace. Large exposed honey-colored pine columns jutted toward the ceiling. Nat judged the building to be at least two stories high. He liked that it reminded him of his realm. Not entirely sure what he had expected, he realized he ached for the ritual of home. Seeking the comfort of prayer had become a necessity.

"Do you mind, Rabbi, if I pray?" Nat moved toward the front of a large but thin wooden bench. The sweet smell of incense, stronger at the front, hit him again with the longing for home, while the rough-hued ivory color of the walls instantly soothed. Everything in his realm was white, or varying shades of ivory. He found the brilliance of color that splattered thoroughly across earth oddly disjointed. Nat wondered if Isabella felt the same.

A hearty chuckle from the Rabbi drew Nat up sharply. "Mind if you pray? You are joking, right? This is the Almighty's house my son. Pray all you want. It's not every day, or should I say night, that I get a person darkening the door asking to pray. I will take that as a blessing. If you have need to talk, I will listen. But I warn you now, I tend to give advice." A bold wink of knowing and understanding accompanied his warning, causing Nat to grin in earnest.

Smiling for the first time all day, Nat felt more at ease. "Thank you. I am honored by your offer of guidance, but first I must purge my thoughts and seek the clarity of my mission through prayer."

The Rabbi stuffed his hands inside the robe's dark pockets and chuckled again. "I knew you weren't from around here. Take all the time you need, my son. I've been praying all day to avoid the work in my office, but that is the sloth within me and unless I get through some of my paperwork tonight, tomorrow will be even a longer day. My office is through the door on the left." With that the Rabbi left but not before giving a reassuring squeeze to Nat's shoulder.

Nathanael moved to the front of the *heichal*, waiting until the Rabbi departed before lying flat on the cool marble-veined floor. Extending his arms above his head to show respect, he breathed deeply. Meditation before prayer helped cleanse the mind and if he sought to cleanse his soul he'd spend a few minutes putting the events of the past few days behind him. He stayed that way until he felt the path of the light wind its way through him.

Speaking *scripture,* Nat started his prayer. "I beg thy guidance, Almighty father. I am a mere servant of yours, wishing to fulfill thy task. I seek help in mind, body and soul. Lend thy light."

Nat thought he must have said the formal prayer a dozen times before he heard the soft answer of the Mistress.

"Nathanael, first born of the House of Raphael, thou asked for this task. Thou hast petitioned for this honor."

Careful to keep his voice neutral, Nat didn't dare raise his eyes. He felt more than saw the Mistress' cloaked form hovering near him.

"Yes Mistress, but they...the Cherub who is to be my heavenly wife, she is not..." Nathanael paused, his gut tightened. He didn't dare use the word that had jumped into his mind. The Mistress favored Cherubs. To call his soul-mate impure would offend and the word felt wrong, even to him.

"They have been exiled for ten years."

"Your point, Nathanael?" asked the Mistress.

Ticked that she didn't seem to care for their earthly circumstances, he barely refrained himself from looking up. Instead, taking a calming breath as his father had taught, he continued. "I mean no disrespect."

"None so far taken, *Sere.*"

He nodded. "Could there have been a mistake?"

Fire ripped through his right shoulder the minute the Mistress laid a hand on him. "Art thou questioning the Almighty?"

"No...no, I would never." *But I question you.* The Mistress removed her hand, healing light taking away the burning sting of her contact.

"I shall speak plainly. These times on earth are troubled, Nathanael. The Almighty tests all his children. Some more than others, but there is always a reason. Isabella is your *b'iā.*"

She doesn't want to be, he thought.

"What she wants is irrelevant in the greater scheme of The Almighty's wishes. She is your heavenly wife, bound by the blessed holy laws. She is the other half of your soul."

"She's not Cherub like," blurted Nathanael. *Not at all the type of Cherub I want or desire.*

"You dare say one of my Cherub's hearts is not pure? Her soul not a beacon to thy own? Thou must look unto thyself, Nathanael. Perfection is a holy word we all ascribe to attain. What is best for us might be the flaws we find together to mend us whole. This is thy task. This is Isabella's task. My daughter is more Cherub than thee have yet discovered. Love her like you were meant. Accept her for who she is, not some fanciful notion you have been taught. Accept my forgiveness and go forth with a blessed soul."

The cold of the empty synagogue settled like a mantle around him the minute the Mistress departed. Stiffly he moved from his prone position to stand, bowing four times—once to the East, South, North and West, as was angel custom when leaving the Prayer House.

Knocking gently on the Rabbi's door, Nathanael waited a heartbeat to be welcomed into his sanctuary.

"Ah, my son, did praying help?"

Sort of. Nat took the offered chair. "Yes, thank you."

"Women trouble, right? By the way we never did introduce ourselves. I am the Rabbi here but feel free to call me Joe," stated the Rabbi, startling Nat out of his inner thoughts.

"Joe?"

"As in your average Joe, but if you like, Joseph."

Nat smiled. "I am Nathanael..." He paused, almost launching into his formal title, knowing that would open a flood gate of questions. "Feel free to call me Nat."

"Well Nat, am I right? Women troubles?"

Nat nodded.

Joe took a sip of what had to be cold coffee. He leaned back in his wooden chair and assessed Nat. "Normally I'd launch into a talk about youth, lust and give it time, but I sense the seriousness in you. Why don't you explain? Maybe I can offer some sage advice," he grinned, as he stroked his long beard, thoughtfully.

"The woman I am supposed to be with isn't at all like I thought."

"Ah, an arranged marriage we are talking about. Had one of those myself so I can sympathize. But let me tell you my story. Maybe that will help."

Nat settled into his chair, enjoying the rumbling soft cadence of Joe's tale. The wisdom he learned from the Rabbi's story touched him greatly, even more so than the Mistress' forgiveness or tangled words of wisdom.

Listening to Joe talk he tried to imagine how Isabella must have felt—exiled from her home for so long, forced to adapt to mankind's culture with the added burden of leading her fellow Cherub sisters. Not for the faint of heart. Then he remembered her sheer determination, her bravery facing down the demons in the alley and something sparked to life within him.

A vision of her softly singing a healing chant to soothe the male, Gareth, also stole through him. Doing only what she'd been taught, he realized. Cherubs healed with their voice and Gareth needed mending. Shocked to discover a male in her sanctuary, Nathanael had invaded the man's mind, instantly soaking up his sorrow and the guilt eating away at his soul. The death of his fellow warriors was a plague scourging through all of him. He'd taken to alcohol to ease the burden of living. Isabella offered him comfort through her healing voice and while Nat didn't like her hands-on approach with Gareth, he did admire her strength of character. She might not dress like a Cherub but inside she was that and more. Warrior, leader, healer and mother. Embodying all the amazing Cherub qualities, well except for the leader part, he amended, liking that aspect of her a lot. Knowing he shouldn't.

His future wife though, would not bear arms. His future wife would give up this life. That wasn't up for negotiation. Without her consent, he'd bind her to him, if need be. The notion made bile rise in his throat. He had vowed never to do such a thing, having promised his own Cherub mother he wouldn't, after discovering how his father had treated her. His mother accepted her position with quiet dignity but Nat knew her loneliness. His father only called for her when the breeding necessitated. The holy binding ensured neither could take another. That was the Cherub-Seraphim way.

Once the blessed binding words were said, they could only have sex with each other. Nat wouldn't be able to relieve his physical ache with any other. The reason for joining was to produce heavenly offspring. He'd become a *Sera*—a full-fledged Seraphim warrior able to fight in the heavenly army. He'd slay the dark stain of evil that continued to threaten the heavenly realm, one that more and more knocked with a loud bang on the Heavenly Gates.

His mother always said live a life with purpose to serve the greater good and the Almighty's path of light. To become all she wanted he would have to do something she would hate.

Chapter Five

IZZY LIKED TO BOLDLY flash some of her flesh when singing in the band. Why? Because it went totally beyond what she'd been taught. While they didn't wear some of the more tantalizing clothing a lot of teen girls did, they did wear short skirts and halter-like tops on stage. If her own mother could have seen her she'd certainly drop dead. Thanks to the demons and the last heavenly war she didn't worry about that. Her mother, like Meredith's, had been killed trying to save her and the other Cherubs clustered together for evening prayer. Izzy had vowed that day, watching her mother use her body as a shield to save her she would learn to fight. No one else would ever sacrifice their life for her.

She looked over at Anya, who had the unique distinction of being the youngest Cherub kicked out of the heavens. Forced from the heavens at the tender age of sixteen she, like the rest of them, hadn't aged a day in a decade. Showcasing flesh was a rebellious act and went against everything they had been taught as Cherubs. *That's why we do it.* But still, every night when Izzy forced herself to appear happy and relaxed in her stage outfit, she never felt at ease. She might wish to be brazen and admire the carefree attitude of the girls who dressed in skimpy attire at the recreation center but deep down her teachings, her upbringing, reared their ugly head. She might feel uncomfortable but not in this lifetime would she ever let on her true feelings to her fellow sister.

Sunday night and the recreational center owned by Michael Hughes, known as Big Daddy, to them and his closest friends, filled with the usual. Once again Izzy thanked the heavens he'd found her. To this day, ten years later, she wasn't sure what she would have done without his kind offer of help with no strings attached. That time, when

Izzy had to quickly acclimatize to Earth she'd learned the hard way that not all humans were nice or caring. With nowhere to go she'd quite literally had to sing for her supper. Humans called it begging but it had never felt degrading to Izzy, but it also wasn't always fun.

Michael had discovered her a month later after she'd left the caring hands of humans who tried to heal her. It had been a cold, drizzle day and she'd feared her voice might give out. Singing on a busy downtown corner, Michael had walked up to her and handed her a business card. Their hands had touched briefly, but it was all Izzy needed to grasp the intel she'd needed. Michael wanted to help teens. He'd suffered his own loss and when the heavens opened up that night with a heavy downpour Izzy took him up on his offer of help.

Over the years the center had changed, with her help and that of her sisters she'd rescued. Luckily, Michael never once said no to her. He had inherited what he called "old money," and thoroughly liked trying to make a difference. She knew he had hopes of setting her and the band up with a "lucrative" record deal. Izzy wanted none of that. In exchange for the brownstone he and her sister's had helped refurbish, they sang and did other chores as needed for the center.

Izzy liked performing on Sunday nights. The crowds were less interested in scoring sex, or looking tough. Most of the teens crossing Michael's door were like her, in need. Sunday nights was more a night out with friends, a last hurrah before the week of school called them forth.

Tonight Izzy knew she showed a lot more flesh than usual. She'd discarded her normal high-top sneakers for the sexy high heeled boots she liked to wear when fighting demons and that should have told her something. She wasn't feeling her usual calm, in control self and it was all Nathanael's fault.

"Everything okay, Izzy?" asked Mike, the minute she moved up behind him at the bar that offered lot of drinks but no alcohol. He handed her a glass of her usual—ice cold water.

"You bet. Why?"

"Seemed like there was a bit of trouble the other night. Care to explain all that?"

No not really. Taking two sips of water, Izzy knew Mike wouldn't let her leave until she said something. "Old friend showed up unexpectedly. No biggie."

He made a move to touch her arm. She tensed, her body instinctively moving out of reach. She, like all of her sisters, was an empathy. While she'd touched him a few times over the years she'd always tried to avoid it. If touched, they could find themselves choking on a sudden rush of human emotions. Izzy had learned to dull the affect by staying out of reach or instantly humming a healing chant to her soul. Anya had yet to master turning off the tangible rush of human emotions. Tonight, like most nights, she lay quietly in her bed reading poetry. Currently she was engrossed in Josephine Balmer's, *Sappho-Poems and Fragments*. Izzy knew eventually she'd have to get the *novice* to face the real world. She'd tried in the past to get Anya to sing, knowing evoking her musical voice would bless her. Anya refused. *We all have our coping mechanisms.*

Mike stopped himself from touching her and instead leaned his head closer to hers. "If he becomes a biggie," said Mike, looking over at the table near the back of the bar where Nathanael sat, "I can deal with him."

Oh no you can't. "Thanks, Mike. Seriously, all's fine. He'll behave." *I'll behave.*

"By the way, nice outfit," said Mike, giving her a friendly wink.

"Daring ain't it?"

"Oh yeah. Not your typical attire, Izzy, but I'm a man, and I like."

Izzy didn't bother blushing, she turned away from him and made her way back stage.

"You are wearing that to annoy him" stated Meredith, as she handed out the bells to each of the sisters performing tonight.

For a second Isabelle thought of asking who she meant, but why play stupid. All of them scented the Seraphim the minute his heavenly presence crossed the threshold. He smelled of soap mixed with steel. She wished he smelled like the overripe male teens who frequented the establishment. They doused themselves in so much cologne it made her gag. Not Nathanael. He didn't need to enhance what the Almighty had blessed him with. He was Seraphim. A simple statement encompassing a total male package.

Izzy leaned closer to Meredith. "You bet I am. Maybe he'll realize I'm not the perfect Cherub and certainly not wife material and fly back to the heavens." She laughed bitterly.

"Play with fire and you'll get burnt, Izzy" teased Shea, picking up her small gold harp.

The harp had been a gift from Big Daddy. Shea always played it on Sundays for him. Shea thought of Mike as a friend, but Izzy highly their twenty-four-year old benefactor, who was eight years Shea's senior, thought of the Cherub in a different way. She wondered when he'd clue in on the fact that none of them aged.

Izzy watched as five of her sisters stationed themselves on the stage. The velvet curtain kept their movements hidden from the excited crowd. Even without touching humans, Izzy felt their emotions. One in particular thrummed through her. That edgy-daring feeling invaded her mind and body but she vowed not to let Nathanael's anger rub her wrong.

Izzy wore a white leather bra underneath a black meshed shirt barely reaching her navel. The netting covered the scars on her back. Tonight she'd forgone the short skirt. Her legs, kept hidden in the tight white leather pants, hid the Rashi script inked into her flesh without her consent. Izzy knew she looked sexy. Pissed to the core she showed more flesh than a Cherub should to any other than her mate. She wanted Nathanael to get her message loud and clear. *I am not a perfect Cherub. I will dress any way I choose. I will wear what I think is appropriate. You will never dictate to me.*

Taking her place center stage, Izzy prepared to sing her heart out. Purposely sparking his lust, she prayed he'd end up tossing and turning in bed with visions of what he would never get from her slamming through his subconscious. When the curtain ascended, her stomach pitched. Her eyes immediately sought him out and she hated herself for that and for the fact she'd had a terrible sleep last night. His mere presence had disturbed the calm equilibrium she'd established. No one, especially not the son of the angel who had ripped off her wings, was going to get away with that.

FURY UNCOILED IN A swift bolt through Nathanael. He couldn't believe his eyes. *What is she thinking?* His gut told him she knew exactly what she did. Openly displaying her body, flashing her skin, the cleavage of her breasts swelled temptingly more with each breath she took into her lungs. Her breasts were barely restrained in the tight bra totally visible behind the meshed shirt. *If that shirt is supposed to conceal, it failed.* He clenched his jaw so hard his mouth began to hurt.

Anger ripped through him. He wouldn't be surprised if he found himself levitating—the one heavenly power he'd kept in this realm. Thankful now that the Mistress in her wisdom had removed his wings as a temporary measure, Nat knew if he'd had he his wings he'd fly to the stage and sweep her away. Rational, Seraphim common sense flew to the heavens the minute he'd spied his Isabella, and make no mistake she was and would be his. First, she'd had the nerve to cozy up to the manager. The same cursed human who had given him that unholy drink the other night. Nat felt his teeth gnash together, again, while his fist clenched tightly. He didn't like how comfortable she appeared to be with the man. The only thing that had saved Isabella from him making a scene had been her side-step away from the human the minute the male tried to touch her. If one finger from that man touched her velvet soft skin Nat knew he'd kill him.

To add insult, Isabella had sung a blatant Cherub lover's song. Nat knew he was being put in his place by her voice. His toned-body quivered like a thousand hands had caressed his skin. He might have even drooled. Lust, a potent emotion, seized his limbs, and he didn't like the lack of control he possessed with his own body. Feeling edgy, he'd made his way from the table he'd been sitting at to stand against the wall, more in the shadow so he could observe her while also reclaiming his body's dignity. The jeans he wore felt even more restrictive than the other night and for a second he wondered if this was how his brethren felt when next to their mates. Probably not. For one, he might be filled with lust but that dark feeling, like he wanted to throttle his mate, was most certainly not normal.

Nat waited until his heart stopped galloping like he was flying on a heavenly Pegasus. The churning emotions mixing inside him needed to cool. Now somewhat clear-headed he planned his battle strategy. And a battle it was. Probably the toughest one of his life.

Still feeling the lingering affects of her sensual voice, he had yet to vanquish the image of the graphic words that had rolled off her tongue with a lover's skill—explicit words that teased every Seraphim cell. By the holiest of holy relics, he was somewhat appeased knowing none of the humans understood a word. *They are lucky.* At first when Isabella had teased him with her attire he'd been shocked. She stepped over the line, playing and flirting with him through her songs. Tonight he planned to also join in on her idea of fun. Only he'd be the one stroking her fire.

Let's see who wins this round.

Nat didn't knock when he came to Isabella's bedroom door, her sanctuary. He didn't ask permission either from her fellow Cherub sisters, who graciously backed away to allow him to march upstairs. He was Seraphim and Cherubs were meant to serve. It was the way of their culture. Exerting male confidence as his due, he strolled into Isabella's private sanctuary, opened the door to her private bath and almost fell to his knees.

Naked, only tiny bursting bubbles covered her flesh. Her Cherub scent sailed into his senses. Everything about her matched his desires. Her scent, a combination of fresh *Illa'um* flowers that grew in the heavenly gardens mixed with sensual innocence, the golden-hue of her svelte body and even her sensual voice—all had been created for him.

Isabella gasped. Outrage, anger and astonishment made her pretty flesh pinkish. Nat grinned. She hadn't thought him Seraphim enough to confront her. The element of surprise might work in his favor.

Mastering his lust that had instantly boiled back, thicker then the blessed red wine, with calm and ease Nat perched his fully-clothed body on the side of her large oval bath. He waited.

His eyes riveted to the *Rashi* markings curving around her thighs. By the path of light and all the scribes, the sight of those tattoos seize him. He didn't dare shift his weight on his perch, knowing by the narrowing of her lids she assessed him. Cherub's were supposed to be unblemished. Seeing her inked flesh, like looking at a holy painting, moved him deeply. He longed to trace each semi curve of the ancient lettering or better yet let his tongue lick its way from thigh to knee and even higher.

"Get out now. This is indecent!"

Her voice lowed to a barely restrained scream as she whispered at him through her clenched teeth. Her arms crossed over her chest, a feeble attempt at modesty.

"Indecent," he rasped, leaning more over the side of the tub. "Let us talk about the meaning of that word *b'iā*." His voice, a dead whisper of calm before a storm, caused her light blue eyes to widen in registered shock.

He meant business. A moment's regret for her rebellious actions sprinkled through her like the orange-red sacred sands of *Mount Ch'rb*, her homeland. She had pushed this Seraphim too far. She'd thought by teasing him he'd leave in disgust. Instead, a geyser of volcanic heavenly power wrapped with determination was reflected in the turbulent grays of his eyes.

Isabella didn't know how to uncompromise herself. Naked, he had every right to look upon her flesh. He was her soul-mate. His bold, hot, assessing appraisal told her this was no mere *Sere*. He looked nineteen, the youth of his skin glowing golden. The cheeks of his face slightly flushed with his undisclosed discovery. Part of her liked his reaction to her and part despised that line of thinking.

"You shouldn't be in here?" She hated the quiver in her voice.

He leaned his head closer. She attempted to sink lower into the now cooling tub of water.

"I shouldn't," he mocked. "By the path of light, who should be here?"

Isabella sputtered, something she never did. "That's not what I meant and you know it."

"I know nothing of the sort, Isabella. I do not know you and tonight you made it blatantly clear you do not know me. Did you think your actions and sinful voice would repulse me? Ah, I can see you did. You are my—"

"Don't say it. I can't stand that word."

"Then what shall I call you? Are you telling me you feel nothing for me? I know I certainly feel something, something I've never felt before."

Isabella watched his hand approach the foam of bubbles. Everything in her grew taut, anticipation, desire and passion formed shimmering waves of awareness. Maybe she had pushed him because she wanted what he offered. *No, I do not.*

He wet his lips, the move drawing her eyes to his perfectly sculptured mouth. Too masculine to be pretty, his lips were plump and a dark rosy red. Simple attire graced his frame, blue jeans, and black t-shirt. He'd had a dress coat over that earlier but that was probably lying on her floor or worse, her bed.

"Tell me you feel nothing," he whispered.

She froze, letting his finger trail down her exposed neck, past her collarbone to slide back up.

"Nothing," she rasped.

"Liar." He tisked, but his eyes never once left her flesh. "Not a Cherub quality, but then again I think you, Isabella, take great delight in debunking the Cherub way. Am I correct?"

Sucking in her breath, Izzy glared at him. "Get your hands off me."

"You refuse my touch, *b'iā*?"

"No...I mean yes. And I told you not to call me that."

His other hand snaked into the water, catching her further off-guard. The minute his finger touched her thigh, she knew he toyed with her. His eyes zoned in on hers, while his finger scrolled lightly over her inked flesh like he savored the meaning of the holy word he traced. Tendrils of smoking passion whipped through her veins. Izzy didn't want this, but her body prepared to betray her. Desire streaked like the beat of heavenly wings, causing her stomach to flutter, her heart to accelerate and her mind to recall all of her teachings. His face moved closer to hers. His breath, minty-fresh, blew across her lips, daring her to deny the evidence that they were meant for each other.

"I like to touch you, Isabella, or should I call you Izzy, since we're becoming familiar?"

He teased her, the storm clouds in his eyes evaporating to reveal murky desire. Dealing with his anger was easy compared to his passion.

"We are not and will never become familiar," stated Izzy, not caring what he chose to call her. *Now or ever.* Storming up out of the bath, dripping a downpour of water onto him she boldly let him soak her in.

Head high, she stepped out of the tub, pleased he didn't attempt to stop or further touch her. Grabbing a towel she draped it around her form and marched out of her prison of a bathroom to her bedroom, hoping he'd leave her, fearing he wouldn't. She made it to the foot of her bed before his control broke. His arms reached around her mid-section, hauling her back to his front, allowing her to feel the extent of his lack of control. Liquid heat ignited within her while her stomach was assaulted with the fluttering of wild butterflies.

"Isabella we will become very familiar. I could press my point now as is my right. Is that why you continue to fight me?" The heat of his words on the back of her wet neck tingled along her spine, curled her toes and evoked more than she had anticipated.

"You don't understand," she mumbled.

His tongue gently nipped at her exposed neck. His hand flattened around the expanse of her stomach causing her womb to clench. "You are the most beautiful Cherub I have ever seen."

"Just how many have you seen?" she asked, knowing most Cherubs lived a life closeted away from the males.

"Quite a few, but none are like you."

By all that's holy, he has that right. Moving out of his hold, she turned her back to him, hauling the long wet strands of her hair up off her neck away from his touch. With one hand she grasped a nearby blanket. Boldly, before her courage failed her, she let the towel fall. His hard indrawn gasp told her he saw the blunt mutilated bones protruding from her shoulder blades. She didn't want to see his eyes. She knew what it would convey. She was marked, scarred—a freak of an angel.

He let her cover up with the blanket and when she made no move to face him he took hold of her shoulders, forcing her to look at him. Her eyes bore into him, confronted him with her anger. "I gave up being Cherub the minute my wings were clipped from my back."

He bellowed. It was full of anguish and outrange on her behalf and that slightly amused Izzy. Fury took hold of him, and only the slight shift of his body portrayed what he was about to do next.

He grasped her, flung her to the bed and braced himself on top of her, pinning her to him. Surprised did not begin to describe how Izzy felt. Arousal flared like a newly lit candle when the awareness of their intimate position slammed into her brain.

"Who dared to mar thee like this?"

She thought it funny he slipped back to *scripture* when flustered. She always did the opposite. *Pleb*, more like common English slang, she liked a lot more.

His raw shout touched her heart. Her first thought, he truly did care. The second, his outrage originated because his Cherub, the one he thought perfect was more than flawed—she was mutilated.

A hurt chuckle flew forth. "Why, Nathanael, I do believe you know the angel who did this to me. His name is Raphael. Your father."

Chapter Six

NAT SHOOK HIS HEAD, trying to clear the tide of emotions. Everything happened too fast. First the alluring, sensual shock of discovering Isabella naked and in the bath. The holy wave of script that scrolled around her thighs made him almost wish for ignorance. She was anything but Cherub-looking. Worse, he liked the way she looked more than he ever thought possible. Everything about Isabella was inherently different—her attitude, her courage, her mannerism and even her body. Why he was surprised, shocked him. Nothing about his so called simple assignment to rescue his Cherub was as it should be.

Now, knowing the abject discovery of the true pain and suffering she'd endured, made him want kill someone. To have one's wings hacked off was such a complete exile that he knew of only one other angel who had suffered that fate—Lucifer, the Almighty's fallen son. Isabella did not deserve that condemnation or designation. None of the Cherubs did.

"Get off me." Her eyes, as cold as marble, scorched him.

"You lie."

A sad smile tearing at all his heart strings said volumes. This Cherub didn't lie. His own father had marred her flesh.

The door opened and a young Cherub walked in, one Nathanael hadn't seen before. He noticed fear in her eyes and tears marked her cheeks.

Izzy raised her head up and instantly tried to soothe the young Cherub.

"Everything is okay, Anya. There is nothing to fear here," said Isabella, giving his body a hard push off her.

Reluctantly, Nat moved off her allowing her freedom to move and cover herself up more with the wrap around blanket. She immediately went to the distraught Cherub. This Cherub, who couldn't look him in the eyes, but dutifully kept staring at the ground made him realize he didn't know a lot about the other sisters who had been forced into exile.

"Sorry. I shouldn't have yelled," he said. "To say I was shocked is a heavenly mistake. I—"

Isabella hugged the visibly shaking Cherub she had called Anya. She sliced him a damning look. "No need to explain, Nathanael. I know I'm not perfect."

"No," he amended, "That's not what I meant. No one is perfect, especially me. I was shocked that your exile had been so brutal. I thought that because you are..."

"You thought because I am Cherub, a mere female, they would take it easy on me. I too thought that at first. Sadly, as you now know that was not the case. I bare these scars with pride though, because I saved the wings of my fellow Cherubs. We might all be together in this exile, but we have survived and will continue to endure." Anya hiccupped on a sob.

"This is Anya, my blood sister. She is sixteen."

Now Nat gasped. Sixteen—a mere babe—a *novice* who had been tossed to the wilds of mankind, and Isabella's sister by birth. The knowledge shocked him. Nat realized he should have prepared more for his so-called rescue mission. Every time he was with Isabella he felt like he was freefalling to earth and often felt like *he* was the one in need of rescuing rather than the other way around.

"When we were exiled it took us a while to find each other," said Isabella, quietly in her matter-of-fact voice, while she soothed her sister.

Nat noticed how she used her healing voice to comfort her sister while her hands lovingly stroked Anya's back in a calming way.

Nat moved in slow motion, fearful of causing Anya anymore distress. "Isabella, are you telling me that you all landed in different places?" His frame rested against Isabella's bedroom wall. He needed to feel something solid, because everything he learned shook the foundation of his beliefs and all he'd been taught.

She nodded. "Yes. I found most of my fellow Cherubs within months, but Anya, here, took me longer. Left in the hands of mankind, she did not fare well. Oh don't mistake me, she is physically unharmed but some scars are deeper and more permanent. Shh, it's okay, Anya. Nathanael needs to know. I have a feeling his stay with us is going to be longer than he anticipated."

In the heart of the darkness he was learning, Isabella took the time to tease him with a light smile. This Cherub was a warrior. A brave female. The mother to all her fellow Cherubs and she would and had fought for them. Nat's knees grew shaky. He had thought to remove her from them, when she was their foundation key, keeping them strong, allowing them to prosper, to survive. He knew after only two days of living among mankind what struggle of the soul she fought daily.

What right do I have to take her from them? The question caught him off guard. His fear must have shown in his eyes, because Isabella, still soothing Anya with the comfort of her soft humming voice and gentle hand on her back, glared at him.

Running agitated hands through his bristly hair, Nat said, "I had no idea. We had no idea. I don't think any of them know that you all have been here for ten years or that you weren't together. To think of the struggle you all must have endured and still endure, I can only say with regret my ignorance has not helped my cause."

"Ah, yes, your cause. I believe you stated that when you first arrived. As you see now, that is impossible. I'm sure you can petition the Mistress to secure you another Cherub. Trust me I won't mind. Come Anya, let us take you back to your sanctuary. This Seraphim is done with us for the night and with any luck he'll be gone for good."

Guess I deserved that. "Anya, what happened to you?"

Anya didn't answer, he hadn't expected her to. Eyes downcast, her hair the color of filtered rays of sunlight, obscured her round face.

"I found her with foster parents who were atheists," stated Isabella, coldly.

Nat's eyebrows quirked in question.

"It was a word I had to learn when assimilating. Atheists don't believe in the Almighty or a heavenly being and Anya was not allowed to pray." Izzy leaned closer to him. "In fact, when she was caught praying she was beaten. They thought they had brought the devil into their house because Anya refused to stop praying. When I found her, her body was so full of new and old bruises, that had not my faith stopped me I would have killed the humans. They were not demon-filled but I wished with all my soul they had been. They were simple, ignorant folks fallen far from the path of light and afraid of a young girl who could not give up her faith, even when food got taken away."

Nat moved until he was within arms reach of the pair, standing together, cuddled in their own safety. Slowly he sank to his knees. "By the holiest of holy relics I am sorry for your pain and the suffering you had to endure, Anya. If I could take that pain away from you I would be honored to do so. Alas, my mere words of comfort and sympathy for your plight and that of your fellow sisters is all I have within my power to offer. I would slay a hundred thousand demons if I could stop your pain. By the *path of light*, I ask for your forgiveness."

"My forgiveness?" Anya's voice a mere squeak of a whisper asked, "Why?"

"We failed you when you needed us most. No Cherub, especially not a *novice* should have had to endure your pain. Seraphim protect Cherubs but you were, and all are still, here without protection. That will not be the case anymore."

Isabella huffed in annoyance. "Oh no you don't, Seraphim. I protect us."

Looking up into Isabella's blue eyes he said, "You did not protect her."

"Low blow, even for you *Sere*. I told you I couldn't find her."

Nat nodded. "What you did Isabella still amazes me, but this is not the way of things. I am here now and it looks like I will be staying awhile. I shall bow my head in prayer and ask the Mistress to send more Seraphim to earth to help guard you."

"What?" They spoke in unison. One outraged the other with a note of hope.

"We can not change our destiny, Isabella."

"And what destiny do you have, Nathanael?" asked Isabella, drawing the blanket even tighter over her damp skin. "Go back to your realm. We have endured and will continue. This is not your fight."

"My brave heavenly wife. My job is to protect you and I now pledge my life essence to protecting all your sisters. What is yours is mine and what is mine is yours."

"Stop that. Not another word."

"Izzy, let him. Let him pray to the Mistress. I pray every day to her for help."

"You do?" asked Isabella, looking even more astonished.

"Yes. Don't you?"

Isabella unhooked her arms from her younger sister and moved toward the door. Opening it she said. "It's been a long night. You need to sleep Anya. Please go to your room now. And you, Nathanael I will talk you tomorrow."

She dismissed them because she didn't want to answer Anya's question. It was a tactic Nathanael's mother often used when the truth hurt to speak aloud. Nathanael waited until Anya left the room before invading Isabella's space once again. "You do pray, right?"

Her eyes frosted, reminding him of the crystal clear ponds near his winter residence in the *K'lista Mountains*.

"Oh, I pray all right, just not like you think."

He wanted to take her into his arms, shelter her from the pain and hardship she'd had to endure. He felt honored she'd told him much of what had happened to them but he knew she kept more close to her heart and soul.

"It is good to pray for the Mistress' forgiveness. It will ease the soul and help your penance."

She sputtered and then her voice grew as hard as steel, her tone sharp and deadly. "I pray every day she burns in Hell."

Chapter Seven

THREE QUICK RAPS ON the common room door informed Meredith that it was Mike who wanted into their sanctuary. He'd taken to the fast knocks to let the others know it was him. Meredith smiled, feeling the tension drain from her. For a human she liked Mike. He established his own code of working with them after discovering they all locked their doors at all hours of the day and usually didn't answer.

"Meredith, is everything all right?" Mike asked when she opened the door.

Meredith was glad now she'd immediately changed her attire from tramp-like on stage to her usual old-fashion chaste look. The minute they all completed their performances, they always shimmed out of the form fitting clothing to their more casual wear. Tonight a long white gown flowed down to her bare feet.

"This isn't a good time, Mike."

When a roar broke out from the direction of Isabella's room it took Meredith's strong arm from making him bolt to investigate. She could tell by his startled eyes he found her strength a shocker. Meredith wondered if he'd asked questions, but knew in all likelihood he wouldn't. Isabella had assured them all, that Mike would not pry into their past lives and over the years he'd kept that promise. For a second, Meredith wondered what it would take to make him see them for who they truly were. The range of emotions and vivid images that flashed in Meredith's mind just from touching Mike caused Meredith to take a step back. She had to let go of him or she'd end up disgracing herself with a dead faint.

Not sure if he heard her gasp, it was Mike who helped her to the sofa. "Are you okay?"

Not now. The better question is, are you? Meredith gave a small nod and wisely kept her mouth shut.

Mike ran into the nearby kitchen. She heard the tap and was ever grateful for the glass of cold water he brought to her.

"Is everything all right?" asked Mike.

Meredith knew he wasn't asking about her anymore rather the unusually loud voices coming from the end of the hall where Izzy's room was located. "This does not concern you. All will be as it should. It would be best for you to leave Mike.

"Cut that crap, Meredith."

"Maybe he should stay, sister," said Shea.

Meredith watched Mike turn his head toward the open door. She didn't miss the bold wink he aimed at Shea. Shea, with her golden-hued skin, blushed a beautiful shade of cinnamon. Of all the sisters, Shea was the one Meredith didn't understand the most. She was honest and forthcoming, while equally shy, but Meredith always felt like she kept a secret close to her heart.

Taking another sip of the refreshing drink, she forced her mind from Shea to what was happening. Mike moved back into the kitchen and returned with two glasses of water. He handed one to Shea, who Meredith now realized was carrying her harp. Of all the sisters, it was Shea who was the virtuoso of a musician. She had the ability to play any instrument she picked up. The day she'd confessed to Mike how she longed to feel the hard steel strings of a harp, her eyes had filled with sadness, making Meredith recall that none of them were finding adaptation to earth easy.

Meredith knew it had been Mike who had bought her the harp Shea carried lovingly in her arms. She had cried tears of joy when she'd found the harp on her door. She carefully took the spot next to Mike, ensuring her white robe covered all of her flesh. Meredith almost gave into a laugh. Shea and the rest of them had showed enough flesh on stage tonight to ensure Mike knew exactly what Shea covered up under her pristine robe.

Meredith observed the little conversation taking place in the common room. Whenever Shea came near Mike, the big guy, their protector, got tongue-tied. Charming, but over the coming years Meredith had started to feel sorry for him. Shea was eight years his junior, a mere teenager with the body of a woman but not world wise.

Finishing her glass, Meredith rose. She knew Mike would never give into the lust he felt for Shea. From what she'd felt when she'd touched him, he was disgusted with his thoughts of Shea, thinking one moment she was a teen but also nothing how womanly she acted. A part of him kept waiting for her to age, and that's what bothered Meredith. Mike didn't pry because she knew he feared the telling of a truth he couldn't or wouldn't accept. He'd already endured watching his sister be murdered by what he referred to as a demon, whom the police had called a crazed drug-induced teen, but Mike's mind hadn't lied. It had been a demon who had taken his sister's life and Meredith wondered if Izzy knew and if that was why she'd taken his offer of shelter for them all.

Meredith moved toward the kitchen but not before casting a chastising look at Shea. "Fine, you may stay, but do not interfere with Isabella tonight. She must deal with this on her own."

Meredith knew Mike didn't like the sound of that, but he certainly liked being in Shea's company, so he settled back into the sofa.

"May I make you some tea?" asked Shea, casting Mike a shy look.

For a second Meredith wondered if Shea knew the effect she had on the big man. She sighed. *Highly doubtful.*

"Please," he said, meaning it more than she knew.

A loud knock on the front door caused Meredith to turn a quick glance at Mike. He gave a small grin and then moved to his feet. .

"Sure, not a problem. I'll get it," said Mike, opening the door.

"Hi, where's Izzy?"

Holding the door partial open he said, "In her room."

"Great."

Meredith could only watch as Gareth attempted to move pass Mike. Their protector did his job by placing his large bulk between the door and the room, sheltering them.

"Sorry, man, not tonight," said Mike.

"Says, who?" asked Gareth.

Gareth bounced on the balls of his feet, his fists kept clenching and his eyes shifted uneasily to the side to avoid Mike's hard stare, while trying to search the common room for Izzy.

Meredith knew she had to do something. The two guys looked ready for a fight and that most certainly would not do at all.

Gareth quickly composed himself, straightening his wide shoulders and moving into his at-ease casual military stance. It was a move Meredith had grown accustomed to watching him do when he tried to find his balance and fight the need for the liquid poison that helped ease his misery.

"Izzy told me to talk with Meredith if any of you gave me trouble about seeing her," he said, his voice dropping an octave, a clear indication to Meredith how much in need he was.

Meredith sneaked her head out of the almost closed door, and calmly ushered Mike out of the way. "Gareth, Izzy can not see you tonight but...but I would like to speak with you."

Mike's eyes widened. Meredith knew her actions tonight might very well save Gareth from giving into the urge to get a drink, and Mike also knew it. Gareth and Mike had known each since childhood and it had been Mike who'd offered Gareth a job as a bouncer at the recreational center. For a moment Meredith wondered if Gareth had told Mike about his tour of duty. She doubted it. The two men, who might have been close as children, had also grown apart as adults. The war Gareth had been involved in had changed him drastically just as much, thought Izzy, as Mike witnessing his sister being killed by a demon. It was a shame neither men opened up because Meredith knew keeping secrets was dangerous for both the soul and the heart.

"Let me serve you both tea," said Shea, making a move for the large stainless steel kitchen.

"Mind if I help?" asked Mike.

Shea nodded, flashed a hesitant smile in his direction and then motioned for him to follow.

"Great, glad that moron's gone," snarled Gareth.

Gareth's nervous energy flowed like a swirl of tropical colors around him. Meredith closed her eyes for comfort, feeling his fight. Of all the men who had attempted to breech their sanctuary with charm, money and muscle it had been an ex-thief, an ex-military man, who had chiseled down Izzy's defenses. Meredith knew why. Gareth looked Seraphim. He, more than the rest, with his military swagger and muscular physique had made her friend's heart beat. Isabella knew it had been a faint beat and that Gareth lusted after Isabella, but she didn't have the heart to turn him away when obviously he needed soothing.

Meredith knew all about Gareth's drinking and the promise he'd given Izzy. "Gareth, Izzy is unable to see you tonight. Let me be the one to ease your suffering." She'd said the words low, ensuring no other could hear.

"What the fuck are you talking about?" His eyes widened and his voice filled with anger and hurt. Gareth reached out to frame Meredith's face with his large hands. The scent of him, slightly sweaty but potent male streamed into Meredith. A lot taller than her he loomed over her, demanding an answer. Feeling rattled, Meredith did the only thing she could think of.

She reached out, brought her hand to his heart and fed him the love she felt for him, allowing him to see her truly. Her wings unfurled, the feathers arching high toward the heavens as they breathed in the stillness of the night.

He jumped away like her touch burned. His rejection, a reminder she wasn't as holy or deserving as Isabella, almost brought tears to her eyes.

"What the fuck are you playing at?" Gareth's jaw clenched and his eyes narrowed in disbelief. "And what are those?"

Reaching for calm, Meredith instantly made her wings invisible. "Nothing. Trick of the light," she mumbled, attempting to sit on the cool leather sofa.

Gareth grabbed her arm. "Bullshit, Meredith. I want you to tell me exactly what's going on here. I know what I just saw and the only other time I've seen wings like that I thought I was fucking dying. So don't think you can feed me a line. I know what I saw, so explain to me what's going on?"

RAIN POURED DOWN IN gray sheets, soaking him to the bone. *Fitting.* Nat shivered and hiked his jacket collar more around his neck. Fat droplets of rain still slid down his back causing him to quicken his pace. Two days he'd avoided Isabella and her sisters. Time was a necessity he needed. Isabella's true feelings about the Mistress distressed him. A Cherub born, how could she so easily dismiss the Mother of all Cherubs? A dark voice answered, the Mistress had dismissed her and left her and her sisters to fend for themselves in the wild of mankind. What did you expect? Nat's devotion to his faith told him Isabella had to forgive herself before she could learn to love the path of light once again. She blamed herself for her fellow Cherubs' exile when their own notions of freewill had sealed the deal.

For a moment he tried to comprehend why they had done it. Taking up arms in the heavenly war was not for the faint of heart, and most certainly never a Cherub destiny. Cherubs were lovers. They did not wield steel to slay the demons that pounded on the Heavenly Gates and they most certainly did not charge into the frantic fray of battle. Izzy and her sisters had. The notion did not sit well with him because Nathanael knew first hand the war they had fought had been brutal and bloody. His own younger blood brethren had been killed in the last war and the notion of Isabella fighting for her life like that boiled Nat's blood.

When angels fight it's not a pretty picture, but when they fight amongst themselves Hell might be a better place and that had been the war Izzy and her sisters had dared to participate in. War had brewed for centuries between the noble houses, but it had taken the kidnapping of a Seraphim child to elicit blood lust. Nathanael had been young but when factions had threatened his Seraphim royal house he'd taken up arms, as expected. And of course Lucifer had sent his demons to attempt to open the Heavenly Gates, which meant many angels within the royal houses started to think the war between the houses had been a diversion of sorts. As fast as the faction war had started, once the demons had been purged, it had ended.

He worried Isabella's sense of freewill and devotion to independence might have caused her to stray too far from the path of light for her to recognize the peril of her journey.

Nathanael marched through the recreational center and made eye contact with the owner and manager—the same male he'd barreled into exiting Isabella's apartment. In his confused and angry state, Nat had wrapped his hands around the man's throat and lifted him off the ground without thought to his actions. It had been Isabella who had laid a quiet, restraining hand on his arm. Her voice, a temperate windstorm, rushed with words like, he's just a friend, my business partner, nothing more. It had been the nothing more part that had saved the big man's life.

Tonight the man intercepted Nat.

"She's not here." He folded his beefy arms across his chest, his stance instantly warrior ready.

Nat grinned at the man. "Where is she?"

"Don't know. After you left, she left too. Meredith told me not to worry..."

Nat's eyes narrowed. "But you do?" He looked at the human, understanding more of how the big guy felt. "Where is Meredith?"

"In the..." the man coughed, "Ah, in the prayer room, odd I know, but—"

"Thank you," Nat interrupted, giving a slight nod. "About the other night."

The big guy moved closer. "Look kid, between you and me, let's forget it. But next time you lay a hand on me I will knock you out without a thought."

Nat chuckled and embraced the man, clasping him wrist to wrist like a warrior, further startling the guy. "You can never defeat me. I do not say that to brag. I have gathered that you have watched over them and I am indebted to you. I pledge by the purity of my soul if ever you have need of me I will bend to your will."

Nat bowed his head and then unclasped the man's wrists.

The big guy gave a curt nod and walked away mumbling. "Freaking odd, the bunch of you."

The man who looked to be in his late twenties walked his own path of righteousness. That tidbit of information Nat had gleamed while tightening his hands around the man's throat a couple nights ago. Seeing the worst, Nat prayed that someday the man learned to open his heart to the path of light.

Nat straightened, pushed back his shoulders and marched behind the stage and out the back door to the brownstone. He knocked once on the door, not liking having to wait for one of the Cherub's to invite him inside, while also understanding their need for security. What he really wanted to do was race up the stairwell and find Isabella. Part of him feared messing things up. Dealing with females unnerved him on all levels. He would rather be leading a heavenly army than strolling into a den of Cherubs, all of whom condemned his actions. *I don't blame them. I've botched up things since the moment I landed, but tonight that's all going to change.*

With a minute the door was opened. He didn't recognize the Cherub or waste time with niceties. The urge to find Isabella roared through him. At the middle door on the second floor he removed his shoes and socks and this time didn't bother knocking. Opening the door, the sight of five Cherubs in heavenly prayer, felt like a sweet breath of fresh air on his aching soul. *At least they have not given up the light or forsaken the Mistress.*

Taking a spot at the back he didn't dare interrupt the blessed choral chants. Trance-like the sister's voices worked in unison. The sweet burning scent of jasmine incense enveloped him. The room, barren except for the large wooden bowl of water, soothed him with its simplicity. A stark contrast to the Seraphim safe house, filled with earth-born Seraphim who collected every type of electronic gadget man invented. Nat didn't feel at ease in the safe house, but here, amongst the no-nonsense sisters, felt more like home.

He let the purity of their chant brush through his mind and it felt like a hundred wings softly beating against his skin. A choreograph as old as time, Nat felt time suspend as he gave into the bliss of prayer. He let their sacred chant, their heavenly voices heal his soul. Only when the light touch of a female hand tapped his shoulder did he awaken from the religious thrum he'd fallen into.

"She is not here." Meredith's voice reached into his mind, clearing him into total alert mode.

"Where is she?"

Meredith looked at the wooden floor, her eyes not daring to meet his.

Nat slowly pushed his way from knees to standing. He'd learned to be cautious in his movements around the Cherubs. "Where is she?" he repeated, hating the nervous thread winding its way through his heart. Meredith's hesitation annoyed him.

"Slaying demons I think."

"What?" Nat's voice sounded incredulous to his own ears.

"She's done this before when she needs to...to vent."

Nat ran a frustrated hand over his head, feeling the short spiky hairs. "And how exactly does she find these demons?" His gut twisted when Meredith raised her eyes to his. They were filled with tears.

"She sacrifices herself. She cuts her body and her holy life essence acts like a beacon, drawing them to her."

Her words sliced Nathanael like he'd been cut by the *Kita*. What had happened to him in the alley had been what drew the demons to him. He'd cut himself. His life essence, the purity of his own golden liquid had been what caused the demons to come after him. Somehow, Isabella had found him.

"I will find her." His strained voice filled with determination.

"And then what?" Meredith dared, her voice a mere rasp of a whisper.

As a Cherub she had been taught not to question Seraphim. It pleased Nat to know she had the courage to ask and that she cared so much for Isabella. "Then I will punish her for leaving you all to worry about her."

"You cannot say that to her."

Nathanael arched a brow at her questioning. Immediately he felt guilty for his actions but Meredith stood her ground.

"Oh, yes I can, and will. It is the one thing that will make her see the wrong of her actions."

"But to punish her when—"

Nat broke proper protocol. Gently he touched Meredith's shoulder. "I would never lay a hand on her, Meredith, have no fear. What I have in mind is something she will enjoy but doesn't want to admit to. Fear not though, I will only push her so far."

Meredith gasped, her complexion heated. A tentative smile met him.

"I am glad you came for her. I believe in the ways of the Mistress and she still does too, in her heart. You are two souls meant to be together. I beg thee be gentle."

Oh I'll be gentle all right, after I make her first burn for my touch. Nat didn't say a word of what he thought, but by the growing smile on Meredith's face she might have an inkling of where his mind headed.

He nodded, letting Meredith slip away. Nothing with Isabella was easy and tonight no exception. Knowing she purposely sought the demons, causing her fellow Cherubs to fear for her was not her right. *Making my heart race with anger is not acceptable either.*

What is my heavenly wife thinking? She could get killed. His heart plummeted to his feet. Nat raced out of the prayer room, and down the stairs, dread knotted like a twisting vine through him. *That's exactly what she is trying to do.* If she couldn't serve her penance to the satisfaction of the Mistress, her heavenly soul could be freed the minute she sacrificed herself attempting to kill a demon. If she died before he found her, Nat knew he would be alone for eternity, bound to the heavenly realm with no wife, doomed with the knowledge he shouldn't have walked away two nights ago.

He hadn't been Seraphim enough to understand he had hurt her when he'd left, refusing to talk about her hatred for the Mistress. Not *Sera* enough to realize he'd been blasted to his own version of Hell when she had told him who had cut off her wings. Nat raced against the darkness, fearing his time dwelling in self pity, would become his ultimate penance.

Chapter Eight

THE FIGHT, EXACTLY what she needed tonight, pleased her aching heart. Nathanael had fled and she didn't blame him. What Seraphim wanted a mutilated, imperfect Cherub? *Obviously not him.* She didn't like how his leaving evoked emotions she didn't want to examine too closely. After a night tossing and turning in her bed with wickedly delightful images of his Seraphim body tormenting her and the pleasure lessons from her teachers ringing through her dreams she'd fled from the quiet all-searching looks her sisters had cast her way. Isabella wasn't in the mood for what ifs. She had gone against tradition once because she believed she mattered. Born a Cherub she might be, but she also had an identity and was an individual first and foremost. The heavenly realm might not accept her actions to take up arms in the war but after all she'd suffered she wouldn't cave to the expectations of others.

Still though after fighting earth demons for ten years she felt she was no closer to understanding their purpose. For every demon she slayed, a dozen more would show up in Boston. Izzy had tried interrogating the human-turned demons but she'd quickly discovered that was a waste of time. The humans who had been demon-turned had no inkling of why, they only sought one thing—to turn more humans into demons. It was a vicious cycle. Before Nathanael had arrived she'd been getting quite weary of her lonely one-sided battle, but she'd fought for them to take up arms to slay demons so Izzy wasn't about to quit her duty anytime soon.

Squaring her shoulders against the pain from the blows the human-demons were delivering to her body, she watched the golden rivulets of her life essence stream down her arms and face. For a moment Izzy got fascinated with the yellow liquid oozing from her face.

"My, this little pretty thing will taste delicious."

The fetid smell of the demons breath instantly forced her fascination to fade. "Don't you demons bathe or better yet brush your teeth? I'm sure I've got at least a mint somewhere in one of my pockets and I'm begging you to chew it before I have to kill you."

The demon to her right smacked Isabella's face hard. Her neck jarred so much, Izzy heard something crack. Spitting, she said, "That had better not scar."

"Me master said you'd be the cocky one."

"Really, in case your stupid cells are overloading your maggot brain, I ain't got no cock." Izzy enjoyed watching the demon, still wearing his blue pin-stripped business suit, puzzle out her sarcastic remark. He had recently been taken, the black stain of his soul still crept up around his neck. In another day his entire flesh would be grayish black. *Then again, he's not going to live to see another day.* She waited until the two of them grew more sure of their so-called skills.

Bracing for a punch to her gut, she eyed the other demon, who was older by a dozen years. It still amazed Izzy that no earth-born angels seemed to be aware of the demons' existence. She'd made the mistake once of telling the Madam who ran the earth-bound Cherub safe house about them and didn't need to be told twice to keep her mouth shut. *If only they'd run them over, preferably in one of their Porches.* A vision of doing that made her crack a smile. The punch to her gut stole her breathe away. She crumpled to her knees barely avoiding falling flat on her face. Her jeans ripped making her see red.

"Okay, now I'm pissed. Those were my new skinny jeans. Do you have any idea how hard it is to get jeans when you're almost six feet and not a size zero in this town? You are so dead."

Izzy jumped up, startling them. She didn't stop her motion. Her leg kicked out and her arms went wide, her aim dead on as she let glide her morning stars dipped in holy water. The newly turned demon in front of her with the comical still-shocked look on his face, a look Izzy instantly classified in the 'what, a girl killed me?' category, vaporized.

Smiling sweetly, she turned toward the older demon. "Now it's your turn."

He grinned. Fear spiked inside her for the first time in thirty-six hours as Izzy watched the dark shadows of the alley morph into ghost-like figures. Izzy did a slow clap. "Wow, something new for a change." Moving more into the middle of the grimy alley, she braced her legs for impact. She counted fifteen figures, each with red-glowing demon eyes. These weren't human-turned demons coming at her, rather Hell's demons and her heart started to race. The last time she'd fought them had been in the heavens and it certainly hadn't been easy. Without a doubt, Izzy knew she was now in for the fight of her life. Regret that she'd asked for this stole through her because as much as she might want to die, she also had a duty to her sisters. Leaving them would literally kill her.

One large shadowy figure edged toward her. "This is the one."

"The one. Why thank you," beamed Izzy, sarcastically. If she could play them along for a bit longer, she might be able to reach the two knives tucked into the holster underneath her shirt. Confidently, she placed her arms on her hips, ensuring her fingers were a little higher up than normal, getting ready for a quick grab.

With four shadow demons surrounding her, Izzy prayed for a quick death. "Now, would be a good time to have wings," she said. A manic chuckle flew from her lips.

When the demons lunged, she grabbed her knives, squatted and let them fly. No evaporation. Her knives simply flew through the demons like they weren't there. The one with the death-grip on her outstretched leg certainly felt solid enough to her. Punching him in the face felt real too. Why did her knives not work?

The human-demon grasped Izzy by the hair, hauling her up until her legs were suspended at least a foot off the ground. "Geesh, thanks buddy. I hate slime on my boots." Kicking him in the nuts, she wondered for a second if he still had any. When he dropped her instantly to the ground she grinned. *Guess you've still got your jewels. Not for long though.* Yanking her last knife out from her boot, she turned around and knifed him in the belly. He roared and then thankfully evaporated. "At least one of you are acting demon-like tonight."

The rush of shadow-demons coming at Izzy made her want to flee. Heart galloping like a Pegasus she stupidly stood her ground, wounded, and bloodied, but she'd fight them all. Probably not a long fight, but she wasn't one to run, ever. Taking on demons was real work. Better than sitting at the apartment, thinking. Izzy wanted to avoid examining the emotions Nathanael evoked in her for the place that had been at one time her loving home. The 'had been' part knifed her still.

NAT HEARD ISABELLA scream. His heart stopped beating but thankfully his legs picked up speed. Rounding the corner of a large office building he stormed into the darkened alley. His eyesight balked at the scene in front of him.

Isabella struggling in the middle of at least a dozen shadow-demons. Nat did the only thing he could think of to get them off her. Throwing the canister of holy water it imploded the second it came into contact with the hard asphalt to splatter its blessed contents over the shadow-demons. Holy water made them evaporate. Not all of them but he'd take care of the rest. Nat forced himself to pay attention to the six shadow-demons he still had to deal with. His Isabella was too wounded to do anything but lay on the filthy ground, and it took willpower for Nat to ignore her when all he wanted to do was grab her and flee. Seraphim do not run from battle. With practiced ease he slid the small sword from the back of his shirt. Expertly he clicked the button on the sword causing it to extend into a three foot weapon of metal.

"Meet me, Nathanael, First born of the heavenly house of Raphael. I pray death frees your soul." He lunged, the sword straight into the heart of the first shadow-demon that came at him. In quick succession he took care of the rest, all except for one. One shadow-demon had moved to the darkest part of the alley. Nat thought to go after him, but then Isabella moaned. The sound, a desperate plea, brought her fully to his attention. Her golden life essence flowed freely around her, so much yellow it could have lit up the alley. Forgetting the demon he had been taught to dispatch, Nat scooped up Isabella, running with her in his arms back to her sisters. He prayed he wasn't too late. He prayed he'd be granted time to make amends.

"Did we defeat them?" Her voice weak, so unlike the commanding Isabella persona he'd grown accustomed, almost made Nat stumble.

"We certainly did," he said. "Isabella, keep your eyes open. Stay awake."

"Why? It's so nice when I close my eyes. You know what I see?"

He knew what she saw. "What?" Nat would talk about anything to keep her awake. Terror, if she truly closed her eyes for good she'd slip from him, made him quicken his pace. *Two more of these cursed blocks.* He noticed for the first time how the humans didn't offer assistance, not that he'd take it, but their total lack of humanity and morality struck him like a blow.

"What do you see?" repeated Nat, his voice choked with emotion.

"I see the lovely orange-red sands of my homeland, *Mount Ch'rb.* My heaven. Let me go, Nathanael."

"You will live." He would resort to commanding her to do such, if forced.

A flirt of a smile creased her face. "But I want to go home, Nathanael. Please...please let me go."

It broke Nat's heart and soul because he knew he was a selfish bastard, having learned that human expression the other night, he fully understood the phrase now. "You would leave your sisters to mankind without you?" Purposefully he egged her on to live.

"Damn you." Her breathing shallowed, her form went limp, as her eyelids struggled to stay open. A second later she was unconsciousness.

"I will take all your damning, but you must first live. I beg thee Mistress with my soul please let her live."

Chapter Nine

"WHAT DO YOU MEAN YOU can't do anything else for her?" asked Nat to one trembling, tear stained Meredith.

"I've done all I can. I made a promise to Izzy never to call a human doctor for her. I can't go back on that promise."

A gasp from Isabella's sisters made him realize he was acting irrationally. He was Seraphim and they looked to him now for guidance. "But what if that doctor can help to mend her? I know you are trying everything. What about if you all sing to her?"

Shea moved forward. Pleased he was learning some of their names, more importantly their trust, he beckoned her closer. "You have something to say, Shea?"

"Nathanael, we have sung to her most of the night. There is no change. What I am suggesting is not the normal way of things, but maybe you should try singing to her."

Nat fought not to laugh. *Me sing? Obviously she hasn't heard me attempt to sing, and that's a blessing.* "Seraphim do not sing."

"Actually, some do," countered Shea, bowing her head, her hands nervously folded together.

"What?"

Keeping her head lowered, Shea rushed on with her words. "My father sang to my mother whenever she felt sick. She said it made her feel better."

Nat noticed the tense of her sentence. He'd had no idea Isabella's mother was no longer with them and again Nat questioned why he didn't search out more information about his intended. It was also becoming clear to him that none of the Cherubs felt like they'd ever get the chance to go home again. It twisted his heart and soul.

"And did it?" asked Meredith, clearly as astonished at Nat.

Shea nodded. "What can it hurt?"

The sum of it had been said. Isabella had lost so much blood Nathanael knew only a miracle would keep her tethered to them. If that miracle could by chance be his off-key voice, he'd swallow what pride he had, and sing his heart to the rafters.

"I will do it. I ask you all to pray for us," he said. Muttering under his breath he added, "Cover your blessed ears."

Meredith smiled sadly and Shea nodded, leading the other sisters to the prayer room. Removing his dirty shoes and socks, he walked barefoot into Isabella's bedroom, her sanctuary. A blessed red candle sat in each corner of the bedroom, to honor the Heavenly Mistress and to act as a beacon to guide her help. Incense burned in a small gold holder, the smell light and flowery.

Isabella shivered violently in the bed. Nat reached out and touched her sweaty forehead, expecting it to be burning hot. The opposite—ice-cold—she shivered in the throes of a raging fever. She fought her inner demons, the ones that dared to take her away from him. Not knowing fully what to do, Nat quickly made a heart-wrenching decision. He crawled under the covers, drew her shivering form, clad in a simple shift, to his and started to sing, hoping his prayer-song worked a miracle. To hold his ordained heavenly wife in his arms a true blessing. Knowing this could be the one and only time, not so much.

Meredith felt worn out. The last few days had been dizzy with a rediscovery of her faith and belief the Mistress would change her mind. Meredith held fast to that but the worry she'd felt for Isabella, knowing she fought the demons on her own made her made. Meredith, like Izzy, could easily wield a weapon to slay a demon. They'd both taken up arms after watching demons slay their mothers. Together, they had sneaked from their rooms at night to meet up with the one Seraphim who had said he'd help. A Seraphim Meredith never wanted to see again.

He'd treated them like an equal and it had been the first inkling for Meredith that there was more to her preordained Cherub life. And when the battle raged again in the heavens Meredith hadn't hesitated to slay demons. The fact she'd enjoyed killing them had made her seek more prayer time, but it hadn't deterred her.

A soft rasp on her door startled Meredith. She knew instinctively it was Gareth. A nervous flutter started in her stomach and she tried hard to ignore it. Meredith opened the door wide, allowing him to enter her sanctuary. She didn't want Gareth to see her worry or tear-stained face, so she turned her back to him and moved to sit on the edge of her bed.

Gareth slowly moved closer to the bed. "Meredith, what happened?"

Meredith composed herself and then turned her face so she could look up at him. He was so handsome, so inviting, so needing someone to love and a part she tried hard to ignore yearned for him. The realization she had a crush on him caused her to falter. She had no right to be involved with him, or any human. She was damaged goods, exiled and it was best for all for her to remember that. "I know I said I could help you, Gareth, but tonight..."

"Shh, it's okay. I don't need your help."

Meredith knew Gareth lied, and even though her room was dark she could make out his fidgeting hands.

"What happened?" he asked again, gently.

Meredith noticed how he kept standing, his feet braced apart like a warrior, ready to do battle when the war he waged was one deep within him. Meredith patted the spot on her bed, urging Gareth from his warrior-stance to sit beside her. She didn't like looking up at him. He reminded her too much, in his appearance of the Seraphim who had taught her how to use morning stars and a sword. Worse, she knew if she asked Gareth to show her how to use his modern day weapons he wouldn't hesitate. For a second, Meredith wondered why Izzy never went that route to fight the demons. Gareth would be delighted teach her how to use weapons but not once had Izzy asked. Mentally, Meredith made a note to ask Izzy why?

"Izzy..."

"What about Izzy?" asked Gareth, carefully taking the spot next to her on the bed. Never in her wildest dreams had Meredith ever thought she'd have a human male sitting next to her in such an intimate setting.

Feeling bold, Meredith tentatively touched his arm. She felt the pull of him race through her body and fought for control. He looked at her, long and hard, speaking volumes with his dark brown eyes.

Slowly she took his hand, caressing his thumb in the process. "I'm not sure about Izzy. We tried everything. We sang to her all night—"

"Sweet Jesus, Meredith what are you saying?"

Meredith smiled. "You should not swear."

"Don't change the subject. Why on earth would you sing to Izzy? Are you telling me she's hurt?"

Meredith's hand tightened on his arm, drawing him closer. For the first time that day, Meredith worried about her appearance. She almost wished she'd taken the time to brush her hair, but she'd been too preoccupied dealing with the crisis to care. Now she did. He, Gareth, made he want to look pretty.

"I tried to show you the other night. I thought it best you know. We are not of this earth, Gareth. We are angels. Well, we used to be angels. Now we're all exiled. Isabella got in a fight and Nathananel's doing his best to save her. He's her only help."

Gareth attempted to laugh her off. Meredith turned, sliding her body toward him, feeling the heat of him press against her. A rush of desire slide through her and she didn't want to fight it. She wore a modest white shift to cover her flesh and while light, the fabric felt restrictive against her now sensitive skin.

"I tried to show you the other night, but you ran. I wanted you to understand. You deserve to know after everything you've gone through.

Would you like to see my wings, again? Or will you once again run away?"

Meredith was careful. She'd stated who she really was but also said it like a challenge, knowing he'd try to laugh it away. But, Meredith was dead serious. The other night, she suspected Gareth had boiled down what she'd shown him as a hallucination thanks to his withdrawal symptoms. Tonight he searched for an excuse, but she needed him to accept the truth.

"You're not kidding, are you?"

She blinked. "I would be honored to show you my true self."

"Fine. Show me." he bit the words out, daring her on.

Meredith slipped out of the bed, moving with the feminine grace of a ballerina, just like her heavenly teacher's had taught her. Then before Gareth could protest, she slipped the modest shift up and over her head letting it float to the wooden floor.

Meredith almost laughed. Immediately, Gareth placed his hands over his eyes. His noble act warmed her heart. While his hands covered his eyes, she hoped he peeked.

"Meredith what's going on?"

"The only way to show you all of me and who I really am, is to bare myself to you. Look at me, Gareth. See me in the flesh, the woman I am. The Cherub angel I was born to be. Honor me with your gaze."

Gareth moved his legs, stretching them out to gain composure, but his hands did not budge. Tentatively, Meredith touched his fingers, slowly prying each one off his face. Even though his eyes were now squeezed shut she prayed he'd gather the courage to fully look at her.

"Open your eyes," said Meredith.

"Not unless you cover up," said Gareth. His voice sounded raspy and the hands she'd removed from his face were nervously turning into fists.

Meredith grabbed a nearby blanket and swiped it around her body, careful to keep her wings arched and visible. "I have a blanket covering me, Gareth. You may open your eyes."

Gareth drew his eyes up, blinking in her brightness. She knew what he'd see. Two large white feathered wings reached to her ceiling while her entire outline shone like gold.

"Do you see me, Gareth?"

"Meredith I see you all right, but I can't believe my eyes. This is impossible."

"But you believe in the devil. The evil you have witnessed with your own eyes. Why is it you can not believe in the goodness?"

It was the question she knew he asked himself a hundred times since the day his life changed forever.

A gust of heavenly brilliance followed her when Meredith let her wings fully unfurl to rise up behind her. Meredith knelt down, her wings closing tight to her sides. With her heart beating wildly, Meredith placed herself between his jean clad thighs. His eyes never once left hers, but the desire he might have felt was banked with dark questions. She saw he wanted answers and highly suspected they'd have a long night of talking ahead of them. Meredith wasn't sure she wanted that. If she'd stayed in the heavens she'd be mated by now, but here, exiled to earth, that would never be her fate.

"You said you couldn't save Izzy, surely your god will?" asked Gareth.

"The Almighty and the Mistress work miracles every day. We are only tiny specks of dust, in the grand scheme of things. We as Cherubs would never think to plead for one of our own. To do so, well, it would be sacrilegious."

Gareth hauled Meredith up to his frame. Feeling the heat of his skin against her terrified Meredith with a want she could not have. She placed her hands on his face, feeling the scrape of his beard. A reminder he hadn't shaved in days.

"I don't understand half of the things you're telling me Meredith, but I believe you. Now, since I'm here, and since I'm planning to stay until I totally understand everything that has happened to you and the rest of your sisters, let's get you back under the covers."

"Join with me."

"You mean under the covers, right?"

Meredith smiled. Like all Cherubs she was empathic and his lust was potent, along with his sense of duty and honor. Meredith looked into his eyes, wanting ever so much to give into her desire for the forbidden.

"We are exiled from the heavenly realm until we serve our penance. We are forsaken. We are forever shamed. No Seraphim will ever come to rescue me, like Izzy. I have waited ten earth years and not one sign that deliverance is attainable. Honor me. For the past decade I have been this age, seventeen, aching with the want of all that was to be mine, but taken from me. I ask you now, Gareth, join with me. Bless my body with yours. I grant you a heavenly gift. Let my virginity heal your soul."

"Wow, that's enough of that talk," said Gareth, attempting to put space between them.

Meredith knew she was making a mess of things. She wanted to be brave but wasn't. She had stated her desire and he was placing distance between them.

With a finger Gareth titled her quivering chin forcing her to look at him.

"This is all new to me, Meredith. All of it. You, Izzy, the rest of your sisters. What you said humbles me like you can't begin to imagine. The idea that you'd want to take me to your bed...me, a nobody and ex-thief."

"But in your heart you are pure. I know you Gareth..."

"No, you don't really, but I'd really like to change that. Come let's get under the covers. Let's start slow. I'm a fast learner but what you're asking me to fully believe in isn't going to be easy for me, especially because I've seen evil."

Holding out the duvet cover, Gareth urged Meredith inside. In a blink she willed her wings away.

"And how do you do that?"

She smiled, patted the side of the bed urging him under with her. He'd be a blind man not to notice she'd dropped the blanket and hadn't bothered to put on her modest shift.

Gareth grinned and then tucked her snug under the covers. Only then did he climb on top of the covers, lying next to her. A barrier of blankets separated them and Meredith knew he wanted to remove it but like earlier the gentleman side of him reigned supreme.

Still smiling she answered, "I can make them appear at will. Mine were never cut off."

"What?"

"Oh, sorry, guess you don't know that about Izzy. She volunteered, not that she had much choice, but she allowed them to shear off her wings so we could keep ours."

"Meredith," he cautioned. "If this is your version of good, I think I'll stick with my version of bad."

A soft chuckle flew from her, the sound startling her. She'd thought to comfort him but tonight the tables were reversed.

"I could truly show you all that is good about us."

"Of that I have no doubt," he said.

She grinned more as he gently but firmly restrained her wandering hand.

NAT WOKE UP REALIZING he'd slept soundly for the first time since landing on Earth. Sunlight, the blessed path of light, streamed through the slightly parted drapes covering the small window. A feminine leg draped over his thigh, and a head with a mass of yellow hair, breathtakingly beautiful like the warmth of the sun blessing them with the dawn of a new day, covered his chest. Tucked under all that glorious mane was Isabella. Her skin against his was deliciously hot and smooth. He felt the quick rise of her chest and the bunched up material from her shift as it rode up past her thighs. The leg strewn across his was smooth and it took a lot of willpower for Nat to resist touching it. Isabella burrowed her head further under the crook of his arm. She had made it through the night. *That is a good sign.*

Taking the opportunity he'd been granted, Nat carefully edged his body closer to hers, while gently removing her tempting leg from his thigh. All the while he inhaled her unique Cherub scent. She smelled a little like the flowery incense that had been burning all night and a lot like a sexy angel.

Rolling her onto her back, he carefully moved the duvet cover down, exposing more of her flesh. A crisscross of scars marred her body, along with the intricate Rashi script that covered much of her thighs, but she no longer bled. Her heart was back to beating a normal rhythm.

"Have your fill of me or do you require me to bare it all for your pleasure, *Sere*?"

Isabella's voice, filled with sarcasm, felt like fresh rain water. A blessed thing to hear. Leaning back on one elbow, Nat smiled. "I am examining you. Needed to make sure you lived."

"I would have thought my breathing would have been a dead giveaway."

Nat laughed. "You constantly amaze me. I am more than satisfied you are alive, but what you went through last night was not a laughing matter."

"Who said I was laughing?"

"It's in your voice," said Nat, watching the play of emotions she tried hard to guard. "What you did last night almost got you killed."

Isabella rolled her eyes. "Sadly, it appears I'm still alive."

Nat grimaced, watching her attempt to move, noting instantly the pain that flew across her face. "Don't move. Let me get your some water." He untucked the covers from his body, and turned toward her bathroom, glad once again he'd slept fully clothed.

"Thank you," she said, meekly, a subtle reminder she might talk and laugh off what had happened, but it had been most grave.

Taking a few minutes to see to his private needs, Nat returned with a cold glass of water.

"By the blessed path of light, I told you not to move. In case you didn't get what I meant, that certainly meant do not move from the bed."

She swatted him away, sweat beaded on her forehead as she attempted to stand straight. "In case you haven't noticed, *Sere*, I'm barely covered."

Nat chuckled. "In case you didn't notice, Isabella, I was in your bed. I've been here all night. Modesty between us can happen later. I am assisting you because you are being stubborn. Beautiful, but stubborn."

She tisked. "Flattery will get you nowhere with me, but I will admit to being occasionally stubborn."

Nat scooped her up, inciting a small squeak of alarm from her. "Do you think me about to drop you? Come, Isabella, you weigh next to nothing. And you are wrong. You are always stubborn and I am a novice when it comes to flattery. Training to be a *Sera* has not given me the opportunity to learn how best to behave around females."

"Really, I thought you commanded them to take care of your needs."

"And what would those needs be?" he asked, moving his lips closer to her head. He felt her body stiffen and instantly regretted teasing her, even as he took great delight in seeing Isabella, his warrior angel, blush a pretty shade of cinnamon-pink.

"You know exactly what I am talking about so don't dare deny it."

Carefully lowering her back to the bed, Nat tucked her once again under the covers. "I am not denying it. Things here are different and I've discovered ordering you only makes you angry."

"Go figure, *Sere*."

"I do not want to fight with you, Isabella, but it was wrong of me to leave the other night. I apologize for being insensitive to your needs." Nat could tell by the way Isabella's eyes widened she was mulling over his words. He used that time to tuck a few stray golden hairs of hers behind her ears.

"You shouldn't be here."

He smiled. "No one will stop me."

"When I am better I will," she said, a light smile filling more of her eyes than her mouth.

"Of that I have no doubt."

A rare, heart-felt smile flew across her face. His heart leapt with joy although that one smile awoke that part between his legs he hoped to ignore.

"Isabella, you will never again do what you did the other night. Am I clear?"

"Back to ordering are we *Sere*? You do not own me."

"I do not want to own you, but to be with you," he mumbled. She bit her lips and Nat knew she wished to curse him.

"Nathanael there is no hope for us. I don't take to orders and no longer feel compelled to follow the Cherub way."

Nat cupped Isabella's chin in his hand, forcing her to look at him. "I have no idea what Cherubs' need. Seraphim are not allowed to associate with Cherubs until our chosen is picked by the Mistress. And you, Isabella are my chosen. I would have it no other way."

He watched her digest that tidbit of information as he carefully stroked her lower lip. The things he wanted to do to that lip made him hate his jeans with a vengeance. He shifted her in his arms, carefully lowering her to her bed. He used the duvet cover as a shield, needing a barrier between them. When he was with Isabella she tempted him like no other and he needed his reasoning. She was skittish being so close to him and he understood exactly how she felt.

"That reminds me," she said, sitting up straighter forcing his hands off, but ensuring most of her skin was covered up to her neck with the cursed blanket. She looked anxious and slightly vulnerable. Two traits he had yet to see.

"You said you heard I was to be your chosen, why? Why would the Mistress tell you I was to be your chosen when I am the Forsaken?"

Nat knew eventually he'd have this conversation but he thought he'd have more time. Looking away from her he sought how best to proceed, feeling like war was about to be waged once again. Nothing with Isabella felt easy.

"Let me guess. Your father told you."

"It's not like you think."

This time Isabella laughed but it wasn't a happy sound. Bitterness and sadness fueled her now tense expression. "You tell me what I should think, because what I think is that your father told you your heavenly wife had been chosen and she happened to be the Forsaken One and he asked you to petition the Mistress for a second choice. Tell me I am wrong."

Nat wished and prayed he could, but the truth of her words cut like the *Kita* sword—hard and thoroughly through his heart.

"My bet is that our loving Mistress did not grant you a second choice."

"Isabella..."

"You tell me I am wrong, Nathanael. Tell me that you did not ask for another. That you willingly wanted me. Me, The Forsaken One. In case you're wondering how I know they call me that, I'll let you in on a little secret."

Her voice dropped an octave, sensual but deadly all at once. And his gut twisted. The truths she threw at him always left him breathless and angry, and neither trait were becoming for a Seraphim.

"At night when I'm asleep I can still hear the voices of my fellow Cherubs in the heavenly realm. Sometimes I'm even blessed with a glimpse of them, and their splendor. It's a tease, something the Mistress likes to throw my way as a harsh reminder of all I've given up. I know my name and those of my fellow Cherub sisters have been etched into the *I'mault* Tablet. I know my crime to dare to bare arms, to rebel against Cherub tradition is a tale told to my fellow sisters to ensure obedience. Am I wrong?"

Looming over her, Nat pinned her to the bed. "You think I don't want you. You think I spent all night feeling the heat of your body, praying with my heart and soul, singing to you to live, that I do not think of you as a gift from the Mistress. You are wrong. What my father wants for me is not what I want. Yes, I asked for a second choice. Yes, the Mistress declined. Am I unhappy with her choice, no. You are not perfect, but neither am I. You are not what I expected to want, but I do. I will admit your difference takes some time to get used to, but I'm trying to adapt. I'm trying to understand and place myself in your predicament."

"Did you really sing to me?"

Of all the things she had to zone in on she choose the one that made him the most uncomfortable. He nodded, feeling heat surface along his cheeks. Seraphim shouldn't blush. *Then again, they probably shouldn't sing, either.*

"Why?"

Her voice, sounding soft and full of wonderment made him smile. "Your sisters sang to you most of the night but things did not look good. Shea suggested my voice might help. I'm glad you were in and out of consciousness, because trust me, my voice might have helped but it certainly didn't sound like it at the time."

A genuine smile filled Isabella's face, transforming her instantly. "I...I...thank thee, Nathanael. I would have liked to hear thee sing to me, or at least remember it. No one has done such for me before. I am honored."

She'd reverted to *scripture*, the lilt of her voice sending shivers of desire to quicken his blood. Her voice always stroked him, but when she choose to speak the angel tongue, it caressed every inch of him, making him feel like he was baking alive next to her lush body covered up under the barrier of blankets. Arousal flared painfully heavy through him. Instantly he attempted to shift position so she'd remain oblivious to his rising passion. Attempting to move off her, her hands gripped his buttocks.

"Will you sing to me, Nathanael?" she asked, her hand sitting prettily on his ass, not moving an inch, but then again she didn't need to. Through the denim he felt her flesh on his bottom shoot an arrow straight to his heart and this time it was Nathanael inwardly cursing. He wanted her. Wanted all of her, and that revelation was almost a miraculous revelation.

"Are you teasing me on purpose, Isabella?"

"If I was really looking to tease you, Nathanael, my hands would be lovingly stroking something else."

This time Nat chuckled. A teasing side of Isabella—who'd have thought. *Certainly not myself a few days ago.* That reminder felt cold when he longed for them to be so much more. "I don't think so Isabella. I have a feeling listening to my morning song might make you ill and after all you went through last night, getting sick from the sound of my voice is not something my bruised ego can take."

"Funny man. Who would have thought?"

"Do you think of me as a man?" All teasing aside he hoped she did.

"Tit for tat, Nathanael, do you think of me as a woman?"

Nat nodded.

"Guess we're even on that score. So, tell me what is it Seraphim do all day?"

"Are you asking about me or Seraphim in general?" Nat settled down next to her on top of the covers but as close as he could. A part of him felt like he was floating on a cloud. *Or maybe that's just how I feel being blessed with having Isabella by my side.*

"Both, I guess. You know I realize I don't know much about Seraphim culture, except what's expected of me," she coughed, "Of us. Of Cherubs in general."

"And that would be?" he flirted, enjoying the light-feeling wrapping around his heart.

"Oh, no you don't. I asked first, you get to spill the beans."

"Spill the beans? I take it that's a human expression."

Playfully, Isabella swatted his arm. "You, *Sere,* are stalling. I'm not falling for it. Tell me and I'll tell you something secret about us Cherubs."

It was the first time she had called him *Sere* without contempt.

Now that got his attention. "Okay, what exactly is it that you want to know?"

"Everything. What do you do all day? How often do you get to practice, what type of weapons you get to use, what you're taught."

Nat shifted and moved up to rest against her wooden headboard. "That's going to take all day," he groaned.

Cuddling down further into her pillow, Isabella said, "Well, if you'd like to get up and leave, be my guest."

"Okay, I'm going to tell you but trust me it's not interesting. The morning, I'm sure as you know, we all go to Morning Prayers, then break our fast with a blessing of heavenly food, then it's either scripture study or weapons training. My preference is always weapons," he grinned.

"I bet it is," she teased.

"In the afternoon it's mid-feast, then Absolutions, more studies, and battle strategy, which I also like and then it's cleansing before Evening Prayers and food of thanks. Pretty much that every day. See, you're grimacing. I told you it wasn't interesting and you were the one who begged to hear it. So now it's your turn."

"Who brings you the food?" she asked, catching him off guard.

Nat blinked. He knew what she fished for. "I have always assumed the Cherubs brought the food."

"Did you ever see them?"

He shook his head.

She sat up next to him, fluffed the pillow up to place it next to the bedrail. Side by side they sat, sharing a moment of intimacy. "Why is that do you think?"

"Why is what?" asked Nat, his focus drifting to her chest instead of the question.

"Why is it that the women are never seen?"

"Why does it matter?" he asked. The second he said it he knew it mattered.

Isabella turned on him, using her hand to push him back against the wood. He felt the heat of her palm on his chest and closed his eyes in sweet ecstasy. "It matters, Nathanael. It matters. Women are to be seen. We are of worth. In case you haven't noticed, on earth, women cook for their men. I've learned it's a sign of deep respect in this culture. Yet, in the heavenly realm, we Cherub, who lovingly slave to cook the Seraphim meals do not get so much as a thank you."

Isabella made a move to yank her hand away, but Nat stopped her by placing his own on top of her small hand. He noticed a dozen cuts marred her hand and wondered about that. Focus, he thought. "You are correct. It does matter. I never gave it thought but since I've been here in this realm I've become painfully aware of many things that are not so perfect in our realm."

"Perfect. Trust me heaven is far from that," she scoffed.

"So tell me what is it Cherubs do all day."

"You mean beside wait on Seraphim?" Nat liked that she was back to teasing him. This, a Seraphim could get to like.

"Isabella, the only Cherub I have ever met before coming here is my mother. And my mother is a blessing of Cherub virtue. She would be honored to have you as a daughter."

Isabella tensed and attempted once again to take back her hand. Nat played like he didn't notice, his thumb stroked her fingers until she settled. "Nathanael, I am the Forsaken One, your mother would never accept me."

"If I accept you she will be honored and in case you're wondering, I more than accept you. But you, my Cherub, are now the one stalling. What do Cherubs do all day?"

Isabella took a good two minutes to look at him and then she blessed him with one of those sun-shine smiles. "I know you're only interested in the Cherub secret so why don't I tell you that."

A loud knock on the door interrupted them. Nat instantly got up from the bed, forcing Isabella to stay put. "Don't even think of getting up," he warned, marching to open the door.

Nathanael opened the door a little. Mike's voice, sounded alarmed. "Ahh, sorry, but have either of you seen Shea?"

"Mike, is that you?"

That damned human who Isabella considered friend placed a foot inside the door. Shutting the door hard tempted Nat.

"Yes, it is. Sorry about this Izzy, but I'm getting worried. I've searched everywhere and..."

"Did you ask Meredith?" asked Isabella, attempting to get out of the bed.

Nat stopped her with a look, his eyes skirting down to the door and Mike's foot. Isabella mouthed a, 'no' at him. He winked, feeling mischievous.

"Of course, Meredith told me not to worry. That was five hours ago."

There was no stopping Isabelle from getting up this time. She juggled the duvet around her body and made her way over to them. Mike stood at the door. Isabella did not invite the human inside her sanctuary. That pleased Nat.

"Five hours ago. Why did no one come and get me?"

Mike looked at the floor. "Meredith told me I was not to disturb you under any circumstance, guess you were busy."

"Not like you think, Mike. Nathanael here...he's..."

"Yes, what am I?" egged on Nathanael enjoying her discomfort.

She scoffed at him, her eyes darting daggers. "Nothing. Give me five minutes to get dressed and then I'll help you look for Shea."

"Oh no, you will not." Nathanael didn't care if he sounded commanding. He was. "Get back in bed, Isabella." He turned back to Mike. "If you require assistance looking for Shea, I am honored to be at your side."

Mike gave Nathanael at look like he doubted he'd be helpful. Nat hoped the guy would leave but his gut told him this big guy truly worried for the Cherub.

"Fine. I'll be downstairs. Five minutes," said Mike.

This time it was Nathanael not liking Mike's commanding tone. Nat closed the door, crossed the room and got right in Isabella's face. "You are in no condition to leave this room. You almost died last night."

"But I didn't. I'm fine."

"Prove it," said Nat, he ground the words out through clenched teeth. "If you can strike me once, you will have proven your point. If not, you will follow my instructions to the letter. Am I clear?"

Isabella nodded, the blues of her eyes turning dark teal. Her anger at being bossed about showed loud and clear. Nat watched her closely. He knew she'd attempt to strike when he least expected it. Discarding the duvet, she stood in her shift. He'd have to be a blind man not to notice her figure through the thin material. He ignored the lust. Battle ready he braced for impact, watching her like a heavenly hawk. Her right foot sneaked out at the same time as her left arm aimed at him. Nat grasped both moving appendages and flipped her over so that she was belly down on the bed.

"You are not in fighting form, Isabella. I will go with Mike to find Shea. You, as ordered, will stay in this bed, rest, eat and sleep. Do you understand your orders? If I find out you have disobeyed me I will thoroughly enjoy punishing you." Nat tried hard to ignore her delectable rump. She squirmed on the bed, trying to buck him off her. He pinned her even more to the frame, using his muscle to impose his strength. Then just to annoy her, he took the time to move all those corn silks of hair off her neck to nibble on her exposed flesh. She gasped, goose bumps clamored along her skin. Nat grinned.

"I am going to release you, Isabella, but first promise me on your Cherub holy heart that you will obey me."

Nat knew she cursed into the mattress. He watched in eerie fascination as a new word got inked along her left thigh. He knew it burnt, because he could smell her burning flesh. "Stop swearing and pledge."

"Fine, I thee pledge on my Cherub holy heart I will obey."

Nat slowly moved off her, allowing her the dignity to fix her crumpled up shift. She ignored her burning flesh. It was a reminder she'd born lots of pain in the last ten years.

He moved to the door, and she spoke. "When you find Shea come to me right away and bring her."

He nodded. "I will find her. Mike is a good human and he will not rest until she is safe."

"Thank you, Nathanael."

"Behave," he said, almost out the door.

"By the way, I never did get to tell you that Cherub secret."

Nat didn't like the silky seductress sound of her voice. He loved it. He turned to look at her, noticing the shift traveled preciously up to her thighs and she toyed with her hair.

"And that is?"

She moved on the bed, looking like a lioness on all fours as she did a seductive crawl to the end of the mattress. Eyes blazing, she boldly licked her lips. Nat's heart stuttered as the stroke of passion hit him square in the gut. He knew he should run out the door but everything about her still him.

"Did you know Cherubs are taught how to please a Seraphim in all ways?"

That Nat knew. He swallowed and gave a slow nod.

She inched closer, the swell of her breasts clearly evident in her sexy pose. "We are also taught how to please ourselves in all ways. When you are gone, I will use my time wisely.

Moving with feline grace she crawled off the bed and padded to her private bath. Nat's entire body shook. His mind digested what's she'd disclosed. "By the path of the holy light," he hissed, knowing she'd disclosed that tidbit of information to teasingly annoy him. She didn't like being ordered about and her little words of wisdom, her sexy secret, haunted him.

Walking down the stairs, Nat wondered who was getting punished. It certainly felt like he was. Between her flowery scent and that damn secret she'd told him, he hoped he got to burn off some energy soon. Otherwise, he might break with protocol and take her now, instead of waiting. His body certainly told him to take her, while his soul told him to wait. He hoped by the end of the day his Seraphim reasoning won. At the moment he wasn't certain which part of him to cheer on.

Chapter Ten

I SHOULD NOT HAVE LEFT alone. The warning to herself left her cold. Shea clutched the dark cloak to her shivering form, hating that it had rained yet again. *I should have told someone where I was going, or at least left a note.* Reprimanding herself made her angry and that energy coursed through her like a subtle breeze. However, telling a sister she attended a Choral Choir for the Holy Madonna Church far from their sanctuary would be met with condemnation. Shea quickened her pace, telling her over-active imagination to settle. She'd lived through worse. It was past dusk, and long dark shadows of the night stretched like the occasional tall buildings as she scurried down Huntington Avenue onto a smaller street. If Izzy knew she dared step foot inside a church, a Roman Catholic Church at that, Shea didn't know what she'd say. Nor did she plan to find out. *I need to sing. I need to her the voices of others, always. It soothes my soul.* She'd recited that to herself a dozen times but still lacked the courage to tell any of her sisters.

Shea wished she'd grabbed a hat. The back of her head was drenched causing her to hunch her shoulders against the shivers. Traveling through the two smaller streets allowed her to cut off almost four long blocks. A shortcut, which forced her to slink along back alleys, saved more than an hour of walking. The essence of time ticked away at her. She didn't like the alleys but had to get home before her presence would be missed. Questions about where she had gone were to be avoided. Lying to her sisters, something she couldn't do. None of them could. Omission, on the other hand, was a long ago learned tactic.

A dark shape rose from the building, its form coalescing into a hideous mass barely resembling man. Shea's heart instinctively recognized it as demon-spawned. Two red glowing eyes, looking like licking flames glared at her and then the hideous mass morphed into a beautiful dark angel. Shea longed to run. Her legs frozen in place somehow kept her standing. That in itself was miraculous. Trembling with terror, she kept her eyes trained on the man. Two beautiful black wings arched him off the ground so that he hovered over the asphalt. His face, chiseled marble, a thing of Seraphim grace caused her breath to hitch. The realization a dark angel, a demon-spawned angel stood assessing her caused her life essence to boil. A darker thought stole through her. She had dreamt of this angel. He'd been the one to whisper words of comfort in her mind when she'd first landed on earth.

"Are you Lucifer?"

A quirk of a smile flirted with his perfectly sinful lips. Eyes, as dark as coal, flickered over her. Then he laughed.

"I am the son of Lucifer, my pretty white angel. And it has taken me a long time to find you. Why are you on earth?"

Find her? He, the son of Lucifer had hunted for her. His admission and question caught Shea off guard. She bit her lip. "Why are you on earth?" No way did Shea plan to tell him why she and her sisters were truly in the earth realm.

He sauntered forward, his feet clad in designer Italian shoes as he hovered above the ground. Steps full of feral grace and dark beauty he was a dead ringer for a model, thought Shea. His wings, as dark as his eyes, added a sensual element to his physique.

"Do you have any idea how long I've been searching for you? I can see you don't remember me. But, I am delighted that the rumors are true. Such delight," he smiled, revealing two dimples.

His voice stole through Shea's mind and body. Vividly she recalled that voice. How he'd helped her, offering words of wisdom when she'd felt such earthly despair. He had comforted her, but why? Shea digested what he said, wisely keeping her mouth shut.

"Now, the question is what to do now that I have you." Eyes glued to her, Shea knew he paused on purpose, playing her. Inching closer,

Shea's instincts finally kicked in. She scurried around him only to collide with his laughing form.

He tisked. "Did you really think you could escape me?"

No. "Yes. Leave me." *Spare me.*

"Well, I would but I can't. You see," his finger reached out, swiping a wet tendril of her hair off her cold face. Ice formed inside Shea's veins. Inside she screamed. He knew it, but didn't care.

Playing her face with his cold finger he continued, "There is an ancient rumor that the taking of a Cherub virgin will unleash a demon for good from my father's realm and since I would loathe to hurt any of my demons, I shall be the one to see the validation of this tale. After all you are mine, as well you know it."

When the words sank into Shea's mind, she opened her mouth, screamed, her note a high pitch of anguish. What the demon intended to do she could not let happen. Her honor demanded she fight to the death to keep the heavenly power of her virginity, even though the pull of him she felt to the marrow of her bones. Her eyes darting around the alley, like a slither of hope she spied the broken bottle, the shards of glass knowing it was her only weapon and hope for salvation. Kicking him where she hoped it counted, she used the momentum of surprise, darting for the glass.

He yanked her back by her cloak, dragging her kicking and screaming to the puddle drenched asphalt.

"Did you honestly think I would let you sacrifice yourself? I see the surprise flickering behind that cool blue gaze. You thought I did not know your intent. Shame on you. I am my father's son, but like him seek my own terms. You, my sweet virgin Cherub, are my salvation. If you fight what you dare deny exists between us I will use my power to take what you are unwilling to give."

He moved his mouth to her neck, giving a small nip to the pulse beating like the beat of a hundred dove wings against her bare skin. The rush of pleasure that seared Shea made her yearn to scream. He stilled, the dark brown of his eyes searching her face. What did it matter what she felt? She was exiled. Doomed for other reasons she dared not speak. Reasons that to this day haunted her, making her grieve for more than her heavenly home.

His lips when they found her quivering mouth were light, silky smooth, asking more than demanding for her acceptance. But Shea could not accept this fate. Pinned underneath him, he moved allowing her arms leverage. She used it to pull them free. Staring up into his breathtakingly beautiful face, a mask of pure sin, her hand snaked to his back. She had thought to grasp his hair, but instead her hand stilled on his back, the feel of his muscles unforgiving. Where a few minutes ago he'd been cold, now he shimmered with heat. As did she. This time when he claimed her lips she arched just a bit into him, absorbing his strength, while hating herself at the same time. He chuckled and then whisked them out of the alley, enveloping her in his tight embrace as he rushed them to who knew where.

Her mind began to free-fall, reminding her briefly how it felt when she'd been kicked out of the heavenly realm. Only this time when she awoke she'd be damned with no offer of salvation or atonement within her grasp.

Isabella heard the Cherub's anguished note. The sound of breaking crystal, soared painfully through her entire system. Bolting up from the bed, she heard the quick fleeting sounds of her sisters' gathering outside her door. With haste she opened her bedroom door to allow them all to enter. Tears of anguish, worry and something much more dark marred all their faces. The only Cherub missing was Anya. For that Izzy was glad.

They began speaking all at once, worry making their voices carry high notes.

"We will find her," said Izzy. "All ready Mike and Nathanael are looking. If we heard Shea's scream then Nathanael will too. Nathanael will find her and bring her back no matter what." *Why now do I have such faith in this Sere?* She'd cursed him enough when he'd left that two new burn marks of Rashi script now looped around her left leg, adding to her body's soreness.

It was Meredith who spoke. "Gareth can help."

Izzy digested Meredith's words, her heart warring slightly with the wisdom of her best friend. "If you can reach him," she said.

"He's...he's in the common room," said Meredith. "I will ask him. He would be honored to help us, Izzy. And it would be good for him."

A not so subtle poke, a reminder Gareth still fought the good fight. "Thank you Meredith. Please ask him. I..." the world started to tilt, Izzy grabbed at the sleeve of the sister standing closest to her.

Immediately Meredith took control. "You, Izzy, are going back to bed. Nathanael told us he ordered you not to move. He would not be pleased, and before you argue, he is correct in this matter. Your wounds were grave last night. We almost lost you. Ruth, tuck her back into the bed. Cornelia, please fetch some food from the kitchen for Izzy and bring her a cup of peppermint tea. I will talk to Gareth and once you have eaten I will check in on you and fill you in on what I know. That is the best course of action for us all. We can no more run around this town looking for Shea than you. Let these friends, let these warriors, fight this fight for us."

Izzy nodded, her will struggling with obedience. *I should be the one out there looking for Shea. It's my job to keep them all safe. Once again I've failed them.*

Meredith waited until the other sisters left, doing as ordered. "The burden you take on for us is too much. Maybe it's time for us to ask for forgiveness."

A painful chuckle flew from Izzy. "She will not hear it. Do you think I have not tried all this time to pray, to seek her guidance. For eight years I prayed four times a day...ah, I see you thought I didn't, but I did, Meredith. I prayed and waited. I opened my heart and achingly listened to nothing. This penance will never be served. We will never walk through the Heavenly Gates again. I am more than sorry I got you and all of them into this mess and if I could trade my life to allow you all into the heavenly realm I would. Even that sacrifice met with silence. Never fear I will never leave you."

"There will come a day when she will answer. We are not forgotten," said Meredith, her voice measured and full of assurance.

Izzy didn't say anything. Meredith didn't hear the Cherub voices from the heavenly realm at night like she did. Her friend remained oblivious to what the Cherubs called them from the moment they were exiled—the Forsaken. Izzy hoped Meredith remained ignorant. Taking away her faith in the Mistress was not something Izzy planned. She might have lost hers years ago, but a Cherub without faith felt like a lost soul. *A feeling no one deserves to live with.* Izzy settled back under the covers, praying Nathanael found Shea and that they weren't too late.

Nathanael wished with all his soul he had his wings. The high pierced note had to have come from Shea. He knew the human, Mike, hadn't heard it, but he did.

"This way. She's down here." Nathanael ran like he was chasing demons. Mike kept up and that pleased Nat because he wasn't in the mood to wait for some human. Seraphim were faster and stronger than humans but Mike used his concern for Shea to help pump his legs. Sprinting down a second alley, Nat almost missed her. Mike didn't. The big guy zoned in on her crumpled, bloodied form, her cloak wide open. She was curled into the fetal position, her hands clutching her head. Mike fell to his knees beside Shea, and his hands shook as he gently, with reverence covered up her bloodied body. The smell of sulphur hit Nat. Nathanael suspected a demon had taken Shea's innocence.

"She needs to go to the hospital," said Mike, cradling the unconscious Shea in his bulky arms close to his heart.

Nat shook his head. "No. We take her back to her sisters. They will mend her."

Mike took two steps toward him. "Are you out of your freaking mind? She's been raped. She's unconscious. She needs medical attention now, not later." Without waiting for Nat to answer the big guy marched with his small burden out of the alley.

"No, Mike. She cannot go to a human hospital. They are unable to help her. Her sisters will sing to her and start the healing process." *I hope.*

Mike turned on him. "What's with all the weird talk? Human hospital, singing to her, no shit. That's not going to help her."

"For her it will. She's not human."

"The bunch of you are freaking nuts. She certainly looks human," said Mike, still walking away from the alley.

"Looks human but we are not," said Nat.

"Great, you're about to tell me she's some freaking alien or something. Save it. Tell that one to the doctor."

Nat did the only thing he could. He didn't have his wings but he had his Seraphim glow, a holy glow he'd had to dampen since falling to earth. "Mike, turn around."

Mike did, his mouth gaped open and words like holy Christ and Mother of God, spewed off his tongue. Nat hovered off the ground, his body a golden glow. "We are angels. Shea is a Cherub and I a Seraphim. Her virginity has cruelly been taken by a demon. The only thing that can save her now is her fellow Cherub sisters. Their heavenly voice will help heal her."

Mike stood rock still, carefully tucking Shea's small body closer to his. "I...I knew they were different, I just didn't know...just didn't even think. Holy shit, how is this even possible?"

Nat dropped his glow to stand before Mike. "I will explain what I can once she is safe with her sisters. Time is the essence. Why don't I carry her back? We are going to need to run if we're going to have a chance at healing her."

Mike's arms tensed. "No. I'll carry her. I managed to keep pace running here with you and I sure as hell don't plan on letting her go now."

"That's what I thought you'd say."

"YOU SHOULD HAVE TOLD me."

Mike stood directly in front of Izzy. They were both in the common room, the white sofas looked the same and the place even smelled the same but everything was different. Izzy watched how still Mike held himself. She highly suspected he felt like the foundation of his world had been tipped upside down.

Izzy wanted to kill Nathanael. He didn't have the right to tell Mike. While a part of her suspected he'd had to, she still was angry with him. It should have been her. After all their years together, after all his help, he deserved to hear the truth of what they were from her, not a Seraphim, who'd barged into their world less than a week ago.

Mike wasn't one to put off a confrontation but Izzy suspected knowing she was an angel actually made him give weight to his words. Their entire relationship, what she'd built up for years, had changed with Nathanael's disclosure and that's why Izzy had never voiced the truth to Mike.

Izzy hated that she still felt worn out from her own ordeal, but she'd leant her voice to the healing chant. After two hours, exhaustion clearly written on her face, she'd been ushered out by Meredith. Sipping a cup of dark hot coffee she waited for Mike's anger to cool. He'd been a restless lion since returning with Shea's bloodied form.

"Did you think me unworthy?"

The question caught her off-guard. Izzy placed her mug on the nearby side table and stood up until they were almost nose to nose. As tall as she was, Big Daddy Mike was taller and his bulk made him look ferocious. "Never unworthy, Mike. Never that. *Especially after what you'd witnessed claiming you sister's life.* What would you have me say? Hi, Mike, by the way the teenager you saved from the streets and all the girls she's brought home like stray dogs aren't human, rather angels...oh, yeah, not really. Kind of like a fallen angel and all her sisters, well they're not really sisters, we're all Cherub angels and because of me we got kicked out of heaven for good. How's that for you?"

Mike took Izzy by the shoulders, the contact startling her. "This is not easy for me, Izzy, so being flippant and sarcastic isn't working in your favor. I saw things tonight that I'm still trying to process."

Izzy wondered then what Nathanael had done and why he had felt the need to disclose their secret.

Looking him in the eyes, she tilted her head up. "Did you see a demon?"

He looked at her for a good minute and then let go. "No...Christ, I wish I had of seen that or better yet I wish we had of..." He ran agitated hands over his face, his emotions swirling through the air around Izzy making her feel nauseous.

"Shh, it's okay. I know exactly how you feel. The first time I saw a demon—"

"When was that?"

Izzy got it then, he wanted the whole truth and nothing but the truth. "Mike if you want me to disclose everything to you, I think you should sit." Izzy picked up her mug, took a sip and sat back down on the sofa patting the spot next to her. Hesitation made him pause but Mike was not a coward. Izzy vowed then to tell him everything, even though it was going to hurt him in ways he hadn't anticipated.

Drained did not begin to define how Izzy felt. Her talk with Mike had not been smooth. *Did I expect it would be? Maybe.*

"You shouldn't have told him," said Izzy. She yearned to shout those words at Nathanael knowing it would set them at war, but somehow she managed to gain control. A rare feat these days. She tried hard not to notice how his mere presence filled the room and failed. Izzy judged it close to 3 a.m., and Nathanael looked like he'd flown all the way through hell and back.

"No choice. He had to know. Now, about us."

Izzy smirked. The thing about Nathanael was he acted like a Seraphim, all straight to the point with no subtlety. "Not now, Nathanael, I'm tired."

He's gray eyes smoldered as they took in her exhausted state. Without any warning, he scooped in, picked her up from the sofa in one smooth move and started to march from the room to her sanctuary, her bedroom. Izzy hated how much his surprised actions pleased her.

"Enough of the macho stuff, put me down."

"I will once you're tucked in your bed. I did tell you not to leave."

"Oh, come on, you can't be serious. I had to leave. Shea needed my help."

He laughed but in no way did it meet the seriousness in his eyes. "Come, Isabella are you trying to lie your way out of this."

She punched his shoulder. He didn't even acknowledge it. "I'm trying to make you see reason."

"Your safety is my reason. I gave you an order, you disobeyed."

"That's the thing with a Seraphim. You need to learn that not all is black and white."

"In our world it is. Your help was not needed. Meredith and your sisters are handling everything."

"Would you have me do nothing? Pretend indifference when you brought Shea's unconscious form home? Tell me, is that the right thing a Cherub should do?"

He cut her a warning look. Izzy didn't want to be controlled anymore. He kicked open her bedroom door, shut it and locked it and then marched with her squirming form to the bed. "You want me to behave like a Cherub and I never will. Why should I? Is it going to get me back into heaven? I don't think so. And, anyway, I will never leave them."

He dropped her to the bed and immediately positioned his body over hers. "Did I ask you to leave them? No. I asked you to stay in bed, to stay in your sanctuary and heal. You agreed to my terms. Then you blatantly disobeyed me. Did you think I did not mean to follow through with my punishment?"

Izzy gulped. Her heart raced and a warm flush cascaded like a billowing cloud over her skin. "No...I thought you would understand." *Not really.*

"You know what I think?" Nathanael leaned down until his lips hovered inches from her mouth.

Izzy shook her head, hating the affect his body had on hers. When contact came it felt like a tease of feathers. His lips, sinfully soft, hovered and then lightly met hers, teasing her with how gentle he behaved. Izzy didn't want tenderness. After all that had transpired in the last few days and especially tonight, she grasped onto his bottom lip and bit him, her eyes burning with anger and the heat of repressed arousal.

If she thought to deter Nathanael he surprised her. *Yet again.* Grasping her head with his large hands he boldly took over. Plunging his tongue deep inside her mouth, forcing her to yield to the passion she awoke. Framed between his hands, she was a prisoner to his wicked mouth. She felt the length of his body stretch out on top of hers. She wore jeans and a plain white shirt now and they were jean to jean, hip to hip, chest to chest. All of it to much for her senses to process. His heartbeat matched the chaotic rhythm of hers.

He spoke *scripture.* Passionate words that caressed her mind, soul, heart and body and she hated herself. He moved down her body, kissing every inch of flesh, honoring her the way a Seraphim did. His hand snaked over her shirt. And for the first time hesitation tensed his frame.

Izzy moaned, thinking she'd feel shame for his allowances. Instead, he groaned with the pleasure of his discovery and that one ragged uncontrolled Seraphim sound wiped away her shame. The sound, of roaring thunder inside her mind, slid inside her soul. His ragged breathing sounded as harsh as hers.

"Did you think to taunt me with your secret? Well, it worked. Your secret taunted me like the plague. I would ask you show me but honestly, I'd rather kiss you into submission."

"I will never submit."

"Then I will never stop kissing you," said Nathanael, who immediately claimed Izzy's lips.

The kiss was anything but gentle. Filled finally with Seraphim passion, it took, it claimed and it demanded that Izzy return fire with fire. Somewhere in the back of her mind, Izzy realized they were both dangerously playing with embers of passion that once stoked might explode. Still that didn't stop her tongue from dueling with his. They kissed like the lust-filled teenagers they were, teeth clashing in haste, hands stroking over clothed skin seeking for a feel of flesh to flesh. By the time Nathanael stopped the kiss, Izzy realized she was as disheveled as he. Her lips felt swollen and her skin ached for the touch of him. She wanted to hate him, but a part of her realized his fate, like hers, had been preordained before birth. She attempted to will her heart to beat normal because giving up control when it meant so much to her wasn't something she could accept.

"Must we always fight?" he asked, his voice a husky whisper.

Izzy captured his chin in her hand. "Fighting is in my nature. I will not ever be what you expect me to be. I cannot."

"Why?"

This was the heart of his quest. Why had she dared to disobey Cherub law? Why had she sacrificed herself for her fellow sisters?

"I cannot." She would not confess her guilt that ate at her daily. He would not own what had happened to her mother. Only she bore that cross.

He pushed aside her shirt to expose her collarbone. His lips, when they lightly kissed her flesh felt reverent. He was doing things to her heart and body she didn't like or want.

"Let me go, Nathanael. I will never be good enough for you." Izzy hated how much her voice cracked but his tenderness, when she sought war, was undoing her."

His lips moved to tease her earlobe. Goose bumps skimmed to life all over her body.

"Never. You are mine. Or maybe you would rather a human?"

"I want no one."

"You are saying all these years on earth you didn't think about giving yourself to a man."

She sucked in her breath, wondering for a second if Meredith had mentioned her role with Gareth. Quickly she dismissed that. Meredith would never reveal what existed between Gareth because she knew how Izzy felt about him. But what Nathanael questioned was true. She had thought to give herself to Gareth to help him—not for love, passion or anything else.

Nathanael went completely still. He leveraged himself up on his elbows and repositioned his weight so he knelt over her, still keeping her pinned underneath him.

"Who? Who was it?"

The hurt and anger Izzy saw fly across his normally controlled face shamed her.

"It's not like you think," she said.

"You do not want to know what I think, Isabella." His voice, a measure of complete control made her gulp. He repositioned her arms above her head, exerting his strength as his lips hovered once again an inch from her mouth. Izzy wet her lips as nervous energy coursed through her.

"Would you have you let the human do this?" While his turbulent eyes focused solely on her, he released one of her arms so his hand could sensually slide down her throat, forcing her neck to be exposed but he didn't stop there.

The challenge in his eyes made her want to weep. With deliberate slowness he edged his hand down until he cupped her right breast and she dared not take a breath.

"You would have let a human touch you like this Isabella?"

She wanted to shake her head but couldn't. He knew. He knew what she had contemplated.

"You would have sacrificed yourself, your virginity to help someone, but haven't you had enough sacrifices."

He said what she dared not think. Tears welled in the corners of her eyes and she hated herself. His lips moved to her face and he kissed each drop that dared to escape. "You think I don't know what you were contemplating but let me be clear. You, Isabella are mine. Only mine and from now on the only person with the right to touch you is me. Any others will meet with death. Am I clear?"

Such vicious controlled words, said with tender passion while he kissed away the evidence of her weakness—her tears, made Izzy want to bury her head in her pillow and cry for hours. But that wouldn't do.

Izzy fought to regain a semblance of her dignity. "You are correct. I had thought it."

"And do you understand what I just said?"

"Nathanael I don't want anyone."

He kissed her nose and rolled off her, but brought her body up close with his so they could snuggle. "But you have someone—me. I'm in your life and don't ever plan to leave it."

"But I'm never going to be Cherub enough for you."

"You misunderstand and I think on purpose. You, Isabella are my Cherub. We will be together one way or not."

Her heart hiccupped. A fear he'd bind them together slammed into her. She could not allow that.

Nat knew he was pushing Isabella but his gut twisted with the knowledge he was right. She had thought to give her body to another. When he found out who that person was he was going to kill them. He couldn't let that on to Izzy. She was suffering enough and taking too much upon her beautiful shoulders. A part of him wanted to throttle her for disobeying him always, but that fierce independent streak he also admired.

Now, however, knowing how prevalent demons were in this realm Nat knew he had to make Izzy understand. He was not about to let her continue to fight them. It was his role. She was endangering her life and if he had to continually remind her death would leave her sisters alone to the sins of mankind he would. Not playing fair when at war was a strategy he'd willingly use.

But tears, those he had not anticipated. She was tired and wanted to fight him. More than anything he wanted her to admire him, maybe even want him. Maybe using his body to entice her want wasn't smart for both of them, but it was hard to think straight when she was cuddled so close to him. And the feel of her breast still burned his palm. It had taken Seraphim strength to remove his hand from her flesh when all he wanted to do was rip her shirt over her head and worship all of her. That, however, was not proper. He'd wait. She'd cave and give into their fate, of that he had to be certain. If not, he might go mad with lust.

The sweet flowery scent of the room, her passion that unique innocent smell combined with jasmine curled around him, and he couldn't have been happier.

The thought of any other Seraphim, or human male for that matter, daring to touch her perfection caused a fury of anger to rush through his veins. Her beauty was unique. The scrawled Rashi script only added a sensual element to her lush body, the ridged bones of flesh that protruded from her back a reminder; his Isabella was a true warrior. Two elements that had come to define her Cherub uniqueness. Not perfect like a Cherub should be, she was much more to Nathanael.

"Come Isabella, get under the covers. It has been a most trying night. You need to rest," he said again, hoping his voice didn't sound as aroused as his body felt.

He waited for her to deny it, instead she did as instructed. A first. A flirt of a smile filled her face like she knew what he was thinking. He smiled back and raised an eyebrow. Still she remained silent.

"I am going to leave you but we will continue more of this conversation another time. You are not to worry. I am spending the night in the common room."

"That's silly. We are fine here. You don't need to stay."

"Was I asking permission?"

She huffed at him, the smile slipped off instantly as her lips thinned. She gathered the covers around her and Nathanael knew she was stalling to gather her courage. "Your mere presence unnerves them."

He laughed. "No, Isabella, they welcome me and accept my role to watch over them. It was Meredith who offered to set up the common room for me."

"They are my responsibility, Nathanael."

"Yes they are. You got them into this mess but still you would rather fight demons instead of praying for forgiveness from the Mistress."

"That was low, *Sere*. The reasons they took up arms might be different from my own but trust me they knew what they were willing to sacrifice."

"Is that what you tell yourself? When I spoke with them, Isabella, all of them wanted to go home. All of them. Can you say the same?"

Silence. It grew thick and suffocating.

"I am tired, Nathanael."

"Good. Stay in bed this time. I will see you at first light." This time Nathanael didn't wait. He slipped out of her bedroom, unease and guilt chewing at him. He'd pushed her on purpose. He'd said things not noble, but words that had to be spoken. He wondered if her tears would continue to fall but suspected if anything she was plotting how to sharpen her swords and words to use against him.

Chapter Eleven

MIKE RAN THE RECREATIONAL center efficiently and just as effective he was avoiding Izzy. Not that she blamed him. He'd hired two local bands that had come in a few months ago, showcasing their talents on homemade CDs. The bands helped fill in the gap. For now, everyone assumed Angel Minstrels was on vacation. That suited Izzy fine. A forced time off, she used the opportunity to go over the accounts. That suited her okay too, or so she told herself.

Dreading closing her eyes, she lived on caffeine, catching only a few hours of restless sleep each night. Almost a week had passed since Shea had been brought back to them and seven full days without Nathanael. That should have been a blessing. It was not. His cutting remark sliced through her heart. She had taken the coward's way—undeserving of her who lead a group of Cherubs into a heavenly battle. She'd take riding into war than facing Nathanael. Illicit, thoughts of what could have been chased her heart and body when she slept. Nor could she forget the feel, so blessed right, of Nathanael's body. She was Cherub and thought with her exile her inherent being might be one she could control. It had turned out that was not easy. At night she lay tormented with the lonely comfort of her bed. She missed what she could not have. His warmth, his touch, his wanting to lead when it was her burden. Constantly, Izzy reminded herself of that.

"Are we rich yet?"

Meredith's tone said she, like the rest of her sisters, was still annoyed with her. They thought to baby her and keep her in bed. Izzy had enough of that by day two.

"In another year or so we will have enough money for a place of our own. We are on target." Izzy didn't bother to look up from the accounts book.

"Great. That's truly wonderful."

Izzy smirked and raised her eyes to Meredith. "Really? You don't sound great and it certainly doesn't sound wonderful to you."

"No, that's not what I meant."

Izzy attempted to stifle a yawn and failed. "Never mind. I'm tired. Is Shea feeling better?"

Meredith's eyes dropped to the floor. "What was done to her was the worst of demon crimes. Her will was taken."

Will? You mean virginity. "Is that the pretty word humans' use for rape now?" Izzy's voice filled with hatred. Every time she thought of what had happened to Shea, to one of her own, one she had been in charge of, her gut twisted and the feeling of bile rose sharp in her throat. *What I feel is nothing to how Shea must feel. This should have been my punishment. I failed her.*

"Humans feel the same as we about rape. Forcing oneself onto another is a despicable, heinous crime no matter the race. But I fear there is more with Shea than she is letting on.

What are you trying to tell me but won't dare speak. Izzy took a full minute to digest Meredith's words and to look at her best friend. Righteous anger greeted her. Izzy nodded. *We feel the same way.* "Will she mend?"

Meredith sighed. "I do not know. She...there is trauma. We have healed her as much as physically possible. The rest is up to her. I...I...I should warn you."

Izzy closed the books and gave Meredith her full attention. Meredith's eyes shifted from the floor to the walls. Izzy clocked the silence. "Say it Meredith. What have you come to say to me? I need to hear it. I need to know."

"You will not like it."

Izzy huffed, swiping her damp hair off her face. She tried to recall when last she'd bathed, calculating from her hair's obvious state of distress she had best attend to that today. "There is not much these days I do like. Tell me."

Meredith's answered in a heavy sigh. "I fear...I fear she will attempt to end her life."

Izzy flew out of the chair. "You cannot be serious."

"I fear such."

"Why?" asked Izzy, seeking clarity when alarm bells rang loud and clear in her head. *Because we are taught as Cherubs to value the power of our virginal innocence more than our true worth.* Biting her lip, Izzy barely refrained herself from launching into a tirade about Cherub culture. She could tell Meredith wasn't in the mood.

"Izzy, she is dishonored."

Izzy harrumphed in annoyance. "Aren't we all?"

"No," cut off Meredith, her tone serious.

"The gravest of crimes happened to Shea. The power of her virginity forced from her by...by a demon. She is unclean."

"Bull!" shouted Izzy.

"That is Cherub way."

Izzy got in Meredith's face. "Do not say that again. She is innocent."

Meredith attempted to place a calming hand on Izzy's arm. Izzy shook her off.

"Isabella I know that. You know that. But Cherub teachings preach—"

"They preach a lot of bull. I will not allow her to think that of herself. I order her not to."

Meredith gave a sad chuckle. "If only it were that simple. Do you honestly think the power of your order will make her feel worthy? Will make her feel whole? This order is not one she can obey, yet. And before you say another thing, you need to know, that there are marks on her wrists...she tried to end her life after what happened. I think she tried to use a piece of glass to slice..."

"Meredith enough. This is our fault." *My fault.* "We must work hard to make her feel worthy. She did not ask for this. We will protect her. Place a sister in the room with her at all times."

"She will know the why?"

"I do not care. She is not herself at the moment and not thinking clearly."

"Isabella, to her the way is clear. No Seraphim will ever have her. Your Nathanael came to earth to seek you out. She saw that as hope."

"Hope," spat Izzy. "He is not hope. Certainly not mine or ours."

"You are wrong," said Meredith, moving toward the window. Izzy followed her, wishing it poured and hating the sunlight that streamed into the room when all her thoughts were dark.

"Nathanael is your salvation. Shea knows there is no hope for her to return after what befell her."

"Meredith, I've been over this a hundred times with you. None of us, least of all me—the Forsaken One, the mutilated one—will ever go home. Like it or not we are on earth for eternity."

Still looking out the window, Meredith answered in a tired voice. "You are wrong, Izzy. You and I both know Nathanael only has to say the words—bind you to him, then you will be allowed back. A penance served."

Izzy grasped Meredith's shoulders turning her to face her. "Never. I will never allow that to happen."

"Allow what to happen?"

Nathanael's voice, the last one Izzy expected to hear, soared through her, catching her off guard. *Well, what did I expect? A week. Not one word. I thought he'd left. Should have known he'd sneak back into my life.* "Nothing," she muttered.

He didn't say anything. He simply stared at her, unnerving her and that annoyed Izzy.

"It is good to see you Nathanael. Fare thee well?"

Nathanael nodded at Meredith. "By my blessed heart I am well. How fare Shea?"

"Cut the formal speak. After ten years I've discovered I hate it. Actually, I hated it then but at least now I have the freedom to say what I truly think," said Izzy, moving from the window back toward her chair. Nerves on edge she couldn't sit. Instead she started to pace around the office room.

Nathanael crossed his arms and watched her. "There is much of Cherub culture I think thee hate, Isabella."

Izzy groaned and rolled her eyes.

"Shea is mending," interrupted Meredith.

"I have prayed diligence for her."

Izzy froze in place. Meredith gasped. *Or did I?* Izzy's heart fluttered with the adrenaline of his admittance. A Seraphim praying diligence meant he'd asked for a good whipping. He'd prayed all day and night and only on the third day of penance would his fast be broken with bread and water. Nathanael's head hung. His show of subservience quickened Izzy's heart. *I failed her. By rights I should have protected her or taken on diligence. Instead I did none.*

Meredith, immediately, as a proper Cherub should, fell to her knees to bow her head in thanks to him. "Nathanael we are honored thou feel this way. Destiny can be a dark path to travel."

Izzy remained standing. Nathanael urged Meredith up with a hand while his eyes moved over Izzy making her feel unworthy. Izzy looked at her best friend. "Yeah, that's right, whatever that means. We did not ask for your help or your diligence." Izzy knew her tone was tough as steel, but everything about him set her on edge.

"I am Seraphim. You are Cherubs. What you all have endured and continue to endure has affected my beliefs and thinking. Isabella, I wish I could change your destiny."

What? He doesn't want me? By the path of light I did not see that one coming. Izzy set her mouth in a grim line.

Nathanael dropped to his knees, bowed his head to the wooden office floor and started speaking *scripture.* Meredith froze in place. Isabella rushed over to him, dropped to her own knees and begged him to stop. He didn't.

Sh'ulaum b'iā erasum v'eder'at. I'slla cuelum a b'h'lo'avae. Sh'leesm o'doult b'iā erasum v'eder'at. Taim'u. Rl'extera. Q'y ut ā ÿ.

By thee Almighty's blessing I take thee Isabella, your soul, heart, mind and body. I give freely all my love to thee and only thee. One we are. For eternity. Till dust do us make.

The words, ancient as the heavens, rolled thick off his tongue. The power of angel speak danced like a techno-song around Izzy, making her head dizzy. To the core of her being she felt the words wrap around her soul, her heart and mind. Worse, they seemed to penetrate the layers of her skin, causing pleasure to rise like a tidal wave through her. The meaning of the words clear, they froze her breath. Tears marred Izzy's face. Rage caused her shoulders to quake.

Nathanael rose to place a gentle hand on her bowed, quivering head. "It had to be done, Isabella. I am not sorry for claiming our destiny."

Izzy rose swiftly to her feet, flinching from his touch and concerned eyes. Stepping back she glared at him with all the hatred consuming her. "You shall be *Sere.* You shall be."

Meredith froze in the shadow of the hall, watching as Mike once again approached Shea's door. Today alone she suspected he'd tried a dozen times to muster his courage to knock on her door. He knew another sat in the room with her at all times because Meredith had told him. She didn't have to tell him the why of it. She suspected he had witnessed the jagged scars on Shea's wrists. From the half open window the wild lyrics from the recreational center streamed into their dwelling. She darted a look at the window, wishing she'd shut it earlier.

Meredith did not like the music and she missed performing. Routine had become such a strong force that only with it gone did she realize her reliance on it. With routine there was less time for questioning, less time for the want of what she couldn't have.

Nathanael had forced Mike to take a blood oath. Meredith discovered that when Isabella muttered how annoying Nathanael had become. Meredith wondered what Mike thought of Nathanael's golden colored blood. And that begged the bigger question rattling around in Meredith's head. Why was Shea's blood red now? Nathanael had been frank with his explanation. Shea's stolen virginity, which was linked to her heavenly powers, condemned her, made her damned. Meredith wasn't so certain that was truly the case. Shea had no control over what happened to her and didn't deserve to feel unworthy. It worried Meredith more than she liked to think.

Moving from the shadow, Meredith approached Mike. "Would you like to go in and see her?"

Mike whirled around, and Meredith didn't like how his eyes widened with surprise. One would have thought having a house filled with angels would make Mike happy. It was not the case.

"I don't know."

"I think she would like that."

Mike hung his head, and Meredith wanted to weep. In such a short time, a little over two weeks so much had changed in their lives. Where before Mike would be joking and laughing with them he now was guarded and acutely aware of his words and actions. Meredith preferred it the other way. Now, she knew why Izzy had not dared to speak of what they truly were. Angels existing in folk lore and biblical stories was one thing. Angles that you helped rescue from the streets was another matter entirely.

Mike raised his eyes and took a deep breath. "I know about you all now."

"Yes, I know. Do you hate us?"

"Hate you?" Mike flinched. "You're crazy Meredith. I couldn't hate any of you. I think of you like family."

Meredith bowed her head. "We are honored Mike. The burden you carry is not an easy one. I should warn you, Shea will never be the same now."

Mike's eyes grew haunted, but his voice was strong, even commanding. Meredith welcomed it. "To me she will always be the same."

Meredith mustered a half-smile. "Then your honor is blessed. Let that shine onto Shea. She will need it. But..."

"Don't bother with any more buts, Meredith. I get the hint. Be gentle. Gotcha."

"No, Mike I wasn't going to say that. Shea needs you to be strong, not gentle. Mending with shaky hands will only scar her more. Treat her like you always have. She must learn to respect herself and you of all people are best suited for that task."

Mike mumbled, "Thanks. I think."

Meredith opened Shea's bedroom door and ushered out a fellow sister. The sweet overpowering scent of incense filled the room. The drapes were drawn tightly shut even though the sun shone brilliantly outside. The room smelled dark and moist, not at all fresh and airy as would normally be the case.

"I leave you now, Mike, to work your own miracle. Be a believer for us."

Mumbling more to himself, Mike paced into the small room, moving from where Shea lay in one twin bed to the makeshift cot that had been placed on the opposite side of the room. Meredith watched him struggle. He didn't know what to do, or where to sit.

"She doesn't need gentle words, Mike. Remember, be true to her." Those were the only parting words Meredith dared to offer. She could not write this history. Mike's fate had to unfold as was written. A shame because Meredith liked Mike.

Meredith's gift of foretelling was never accurate, and she suspected that was why the Mistress had gifted it to her when exiled to earth. *Curse was more fitting.* Never once though would Meredith think that thought for she knew the Mistress had not left them. She knew, without doubt, the Mistress observed silently watching and while she'd also like to disclose that to Izzy she knew her best friend would rather believe in superman than that truth.

"It's okay, Shea. It's just me, Mike. I opened the windows to let in some light for you. I've...I've been worried sick about you."

Shea motioned to the water on the side table. Mike fumbled with the glass, spilling water as he went, his fingers all but trembling. He was the last person she wanted to see.

"Thank you."

Her voice sounded different to her own ears and she knew Mike noticed but said nothing. Slowly she sipped at the tepid water. Clutching the blanket tight she edged up in the bed. *When was the last time I got out of this bed?* The question startled her because a day ago it would not have entered her head. Her only thought had been penance. What she had allowed to happen, what she had embraced, made her want to weep.

"It's going to be okay, Shea," said Mike.

It would never be okay again, but Shea couldn't say that. She supposed she must have sighed because Mike cursed.

"Christ what shit. It's not going to be okay. You're never going to be the same, but that doesn't mean you get to give up on living. When was the last time you had a shower?"

The vengeance in his voice and question startled her. "What?"

"Shower, bath, anything. I bet you've been wallowing in here all week. I'm such a shit. I should have come sooner. What the hell was I waiting for? A bunch of angels trying to deal with this."

"You know of us?" His admission caught at her. She would never think Izzy to tell him and then it dawned on her. He knew because of what had happened to her. Because of her crime.

"Don't even go there. Yes I know of you, the bunch of you, but Shea to me, you're the same."

She gave him the courtesy of a small nod. She wasn't but suspected he didn't know all there was about Cherub life.

"Is there anything I can do for you?" asked Mike, bending down to the side of the bed.

She shook her head. Her hair was truly matted. Mike's earlier question finally penetrated her brain. The last time she'd bathed was the night she'd returned home. She remembered it well because the bath water had turned red with the color of her blood. Not yellow or golden, but red. A slap in the face decreeing how far she'd fallen. Meredith luckily had been the only sister attending to her but her gasp said it all. She was no longer angel material.

Then why do I still have my wings? Another question she had not thought to ask herself.

"You should have let me die, Mike."

The range of emotions that crossed lightning fast across Mike's normally controlled and so boyishly handsome face caused Shea's heart to skip a beat.

"Fuck that, Shea. What happened to you was not your fault. I'm not about to let you wallow anymore in this bed with self-pity. Yeah, I got the whole 101 Angel talk from Izzy and Nathanael so believe me I'm trying to understand how you feel. But get this, lying down, letting this thing take over you is not going to make you feel better. Don't you want to get even? Don't you want revenge?"

She propped herself straighter, dragging along even more of the covers. "Cherubs aren't to think of revenge."

"Seems to me your Cherub way of thinking has already damned you. Why not go for the revenge feeling. You want revenge then I'll teach you how to fight. I'll teach you how to kill. I'll teach you everything you need to know about mankind."

"It wasn't man that did this to me."

"Yeah, I heard that too. Trust me I've believed in demons longer than angels so I'll teach you everything I know about killing them."

"Are you serious, Mike? You'd want to help me?" asked Shea.

"Shea, I would do anything for you. First things first. Take a shower. I'll give you ten minutes. Clocks ticking, Shea," he said, grasping her from the safety of her bed, covers and all.

He walked purposely toward the washroom and then forced her to stand, clutching the cover of blankets. He moved into her small bathroom, the act intimate enough to make Shea uncomfortable. He turned on the shower, the sound of rushing water loud to hear ears. Then he returned to her.

"If you're not done in ten I'm coming in to get you."

"You wouldn't."

Mike grinned and winked at her. "Oh, baby, yes I would."

Chapter Twelve

BONE WEARY WITH EVERYTHING and feeling unsure of her skills, Meredith slid into the bath. The fragrant lilac oil she'd poured in soothed her frayed nerves. *Seeing the future is not for the heavenly faint-hearted.* Sighing, she dunked her head under the water, loving how fast her mind went blank. Like her fellow Cherubs most of Meredith's powers had been taken. She, like her sisters, still felt the rush of human emotions but her foretelling the future, something she had not shared with any of them, had not been with her before the fall from the heavenly realm. That curse she'd been damned with the moment her feet graced the filthy pavement. Like most things, the curses the Mistress leveled at her showed glimpses, never the whole truth. For instance she had seen Shea singing inside a large church with a beautiful smile on her face. She had not seen her fall from grace.

What good is seeing the future if I can't get it right? That is the crux of things and why the Mistress gave it to me. Meredith lathered the soap on like there was no tomorrow. Reluctantly she got out of the tub, and toweled off. The minute she stepped into her bedroom she felt Gareth's dark energy curl around her.

"Why didn't you tell me about Shea?"

He knows. Mentally, Meredith made a note to reprimand her sisters. Disclosing what happened to them had to remain strictly private. Ensuring her towel held firmly in place she moved to the bed, noticing immediately the tremors cascading through his body. His hands jerked in place on his jeans and Gareth kept wetting his lips. Not a nervous man, Meredith knew he endured withdrawal for his own betterment. Part of her sympathized with his plight. She had felt that way when she'd first landed on earth. Ten years later it still hurt as much.

"What would you have me do? Call you? You were the one that left, Gareth."

He looked at her. Always his green eyes disarmed her. They were so unlike an angel's. Rooted to earth, his green irises reminded her more of this realm than anything else.

"I had to leave. What...what you showed me, I needed time to think. Next time anything like that goes down you call me. Hear me, Meredith."

How could he know that commanding her warmed her heart? So like a Seraphim when he was not. She could only nod, her flesh heating from his penetrating gaze. "You have need of me?"

"Stop saying that Meredith, it makes me..." Meredith raised her eyes watching his cheeks blush.

"Makes you what?" she fished, enjoying herself.

"Never mind. It's just that this isn't normal."

Meredith sat next to him. "You are saying I am not normal."

He ran a tired hand through his bristly hair. "No, for Christ's sake. Shit, I'm probably not allowed to say that now."

Meredith laughed. "Say what you want, Gareth. Let me tend to you." She reached out and gently, placed her hand on top of his. His energy licked her skin, goose bumps of desire shimmed to life and Meredith forced herself to ignore it all. What she desired could not happen. He needed her and she would do this for him. Without waiting for him she closed her eyes and started to hum, allowing her healing light to invade his body. He sighed, fell back onto her bed and looked as inviting as sin.

SALVATION

IZZY WALKED ALONG THE sidewalks leading to the alley where Shea had been raped. She liked the forcefulness of the human term. It conveyed rage and disgust. And that, Izzy had in spades. Each step she took had purpose. Clad in her form fitting leather pants and shirt, which barely reached her midriff, she teetered, looking like she'd had one to many drinks. Inside she seethed. Her mind, clear as a bell, her goal to get the demon who had destroyed Shea.

Tonight revenge cloaked the air. She inhaled, scenting the immorality of mankind in all its forms. Four teenage males did a double-take at her as she swayed into the darkened alley. Not one uttered a word of caution. If she had been human she should worry. Since she wasn't, it annoyed her. Their lack of compassion, a causality to the times. Pretending to stumble, she ambled fully into the darkened alley noting the street light had been knocked out. Glass still littered the asphalt and the alley reeked of rotting garbage, stale booze and slimy oil. None of this concerned Izzy. What she sought took blood and her life essence. Smothered in the darkness she stilled and then quick as a whip slid the dirk out of her bodice to slice her arm. Calm, matter-of-factly, she watched the golden liquid of her essence slither down her arm to the grungy pavement.

She counted minutes. Seven. Of course, she thought sarcastically to herself. That blessed number fit with her mood of the night.

Pretending to play with a tie on her shirt she let evil slide closer. Turning to confront the demon she played innocence. "Were you looking for me?"

The newly turned demon-man, full of himself, walked closer. "You smell great."

His breath reeked of pickled eggs, making her gag. "Really, because you stink."

His grayish face made her think of rotting dirt-crusted snow. His eyes narrowed in annoyance and perplexity. He made a move toward her. Izzy flicked the dirk into the palm of her hand, calculating her aim and distance.

"Demon back away from the Cherub."

The sound of the man's voice slid like oil over Izzy's senses. The dark voice awoke from further down the alley. Like a puppet the demon-man moved further away from. Drool slid down his mouth as he obeyed his master.

A demon glided out of the alley. Demon red eyes glowed at her, reminding Izzy of the tempting color of a warning sunrise as he bridged the gap separating them. A gasp, unhindered, flew from Izzy. This breathtakingly handsome demon held power. Beautiful coal-black wings swept the blanket of darkness as he approached. He hovered above the ground as if he too found the road of mankind too filthy to step upon.

Izzy's heart beat raced. "Who are you?"

"It pleases me, Cherub, that you did not ask what are you."

His tone mocked. The degrading way he said Cherub reminded her of how she'd said the word, human. He hovered closer until he stood at arm's length from her. He caught her bold gaze and smiled. Two dimples graced his masculine angelic face. He was no angel. *Or is he?*

"What do you want?" asked Izzy, noting how the chill of the night started to penetrate her defenses. She'd been going on extra adrenaline since Nathanael had claimed her but that had fizzled.

His gaze flickered. He motioned the newly turned demon-man to leave.

"Ahh, don't make him leave, I was *soo* looking forward to practicing my new Karate moves on him."

Sinful dark demon man laughed. "A Cherub with humor. I like."

"A demon with teeth I plan to kick out. I like. Guess we're compatible."

He took a step forward. Izzy shifted her weight, balancing on the balls of her feet, getting ready for anything and everything.

"You look to fight me, Cherub?"

"You look to die, demon?"

"Touché," said the demon.

"Wow, a cultured demon. Impressive," tossed Izzy, waiting and watching his every move, which wasn't much.

The demon bowed his head. The move shook Izzy.

"How fares the one I took?" The words, spoken in *scripture* cut through Izzy's heart.

She moved toward him. He stood his ground, looking deadly and dangerous. Izzy didn't care. "You...you are the demon that did this to her. Why? Wait a sec, scratch that. Prepare to die." Izzy threw the dirk. He caught it, easily, flipping it up into the air to catch it a second time for show.

"We are not all born to our fate, Cherub. I did what had to be done. There was no other way. I tried to be gentle."

"Gentle!" screeched Izzy. *What am I doing trying to reason with a demon?*

"I face your condemnation but my fate is my own. I believe it was my Uncle who said, 'The ends justify the means.'"

"Do not quote passages to me. Coming from a demon it's sick and wrong."

"Freedom, is that not something you strive for, Cherub?"

He took all the fire from her with that one tantalizing word. "How dare you?" she seethed. "Give me back my dirk if you're going to toy with it. That cost me a pretty penny."

A chuckle flew from his sinfully lush lips. Bowing low, he handed her back her knife. Izzy wondered for a moment if she hallucinated. A demon bowing, a demon quoting blessed passages to her and now a demon talking of freedom. *I must be dreaming.*

"Tell me, Cherub, can you convey a message to the Almighty?"

That stopped Izzy cold. "What?"

"You heard me, Cherub. I need a message delivered, or do you think me so unworthy that what I have to convey to your god is of no importance?" He tisked at her.

Izzy coughed to cover her surprise. "Who are you exactly?"

"At your service is none other than, Ash, Lucifer's first born."

This time Izzy gave into the gasp. "And you want me to tell something—"

"Something your Almighty will find very important, trust me."

"Trust you? Charming coming from a...from you, Ash."

"I am not asking for you to get to know me, just your trust."

Izzy had enough. She moved into his space, willing a fight. "Trust you. Never. You took something powerful that did not belong to you."

"That you are correct in, but again it had to be done. The message or not? I grow weary of this drama, Cherub."

Izzy wanted to kick him where it counted. "Fine," she spat. "Tell me your message." *Not that I can deliver it, but I want to know exactly what you are planning spawn of the devil.*

"Give me your hand," demanded Ash.

Izzy looked at him.

"If I wanted to harm you I would have long ago. We are wasting time. I will only ask one more time. Give me your hand."

Izzy harrumphed in annoyance and attempted to turn sideways. She longed to be home but no way was she about to give this demon her back. Without warning he grasped her hand, hauling her far too close for comfort to his large frame. He forced her to her knees. Pain exploded through her body and if she hadn't been on bent knees she'd have fallen to the cold, unforgiving ground. The pain seared her mind as the hellish nightmare he was conveying to her penetrated her brain.

"Tell the Almighty the Prodigal Son plans to return. It has begun."

With that parting remark, Ash released her hand, swept his wings back in one massive lunge and took to the sky. Izzy feared to look at her hand, convinced burn marks had been wielded into her palm. Shaking with overloaded images of what Ash had allowed her to see, she knew she was double-damned. She'd agreed to convey the message but to do that she first had to get the Mistress to listen to her. Izzy knew that wasn't about to happen anytime soon.

Nathanael did not like being played the fool. And played well it had been. He ran through the streets honing in on the lush scent of Isabella's blood essence. It flowed through his body, the scent of dewy flowers and innocence streamed through him, urging him right or left. *I know now how the hounds of hell must feel.*

He'd gone to Isabella's bedroom expecting her obedience to stay inside, to stop fighting demons. The only thing he'd found was a pile of pillows in her bed. He'd thrown all the pillows to the ground and marched straight into Meredith's bedroom. He realized again he should have knocked. He hadn't and she did not take lightly to his invasion. However, Nat's Seraphim etiquette had been trampled on and he wanted Isabella to pay for mocking him with her disobedience. Seeing Gareth on Meredith's bed surprised him. Wisely he said nothing, only giving a curt nod to the human male Mike had previously introduced him to. Meredith claimed at first not to know where Isabella went. Nat hadn't bought it. Pressing the matter, he warned her of Shea's outcome. When Meredith speculated that Isabella had gone to see for herself where Shea had been taken, Nat knew he'd gone to his own version of hell.

He turned into a side alley catching a dewy hint of Isabella's life essence. He ignored the filth of the alley, the streets and the sidewalks. How humans managed to live like this he didn't understand. Did they not know the gift the Almighty had bequeathed them? Shaking his head, Nat knew he had to focus. Unsheathing the sharp small sword from his back, he readied himself. Turning into a second darkened alley he ploughed straight into a form. Catching himself, he took great satisfaction in seeing Isabella land on that pretty ass of hers.

"What are you doing here?"

"Shouldn't I be asking you that, my *b'iā?*"

Isabella shakily stood. Nat did not offer her help. He wasn't in the mood to play nice anymore. Nice got him no where with Isabella. He tried to recall all she'd been through but it didn't help. She mocked him. *Tonight you shall not.*

"We have to go," said Isabella, wiping her hands on her leather pants, as she made a move to go around him.

Nat caught her arm, noticing all her heavenly-honed flesh on display. He also noticed the cuts on her arms. Deliberately she'd sought demons to fight. One could never call his Isabella a coward. The realization she'd rather fight demons then obey him, or for that matter be with him left him feeling cold.

"So, did any demons come for you to fight?"

She looked at him, her eyes widened. "Yes. We've got to go."

"Did the demons leave?"

"Yes, yes, yes, I took care of them," she said, trying to yank her arm free of his hold.

Nat grinned, pulling her tighter to his frame. He used his weight to maneuver her toward the back of a brick building and only when her back cut into the uneven brick did she truly look at him.

"Look, seriously, you can't be mad with me about setting you up?"

"I can't, can I? I believe my instructions had been clear. Stay inside and let me take care of this matter." Nat knew his voice sounded rough but she'd done this to herself.

"Look, let's talk about this at the house."

Nat shook his head, leaning his chest into hers. Everything about her matched him perfectly. One hand pinned her to the wall while the other snaked around to her bare midriff. She gasped and stilled, suddenly sensing she'd been caught. He dropped his head down and moved closer to her neck. Inhaling deeply he allowed her sweet Cherub scent to penetrate his growing lust.

"Nathanael."

"Nat, call me Nat."

Her blue eyes flashed at him. "Fine, whatever. Nat, this is not the time or place for this."

"Really, Izzy, seems to me you left me no choice." He followed his words with a wandering hand. His fingers stroked her satiny smooth skin reminding him of the heavenly warm grass that grew in their realm. When his finger found her gold studded bellybutton star he teased it, watching her face flush.

"You honestly can't expect me to wait inside and do nothing? You might have bound me to you, but I will fight you, always. You should not have done it," she stated, her eyes damning him while her body awakened to the passion he stroked.

"Yes, that's exactly what I expected." *What I had hoped for.*

"We are as different as night and day."

"There you are wrong Izzy. Night and day merge to be one every day in a blessed show that touches everyone in this realm. We are that. You are my day."

"I'd rather be your night. It's got more of an edge to it."

Nat chuckled, allowing the reach of his fingertips to roam higher. He crowded her but she no longer fought for space. Instead she cocked her head to the side, allowing him the freedom to nuzzle her neck. She moaned and that one heavenly note fired through all his cells. He ground his hips into her, letting her know exactly what he sought.

Casually, she adjusted her head and looked at him. "So you plan to stake your claim here? Is that it?"

Nat seriously hated when she used her business tone of voice. He much preferred her moaning or groaning. He took a step back from her, his arm still pinning her in place and assessed her. *She is challenging me.* His eyes roamed freely over her, lingering with delight on the swell of her cleavage.

"As my *b'iā* you will never dress like that again." He fought not to grin. Playing with the tail of a lioness not for the faint hearted.

Her eyes widened and she cursed a blue streak at him. When she gasped this time it had nothing to do with pleasure and a lot to do with the pain from the Rashi script burning into her flesh. Deliciously he wondered where it all ended up.

"I am not your *b'ïä.*"

"You dare deny the words I have said with the blessing of the Almighty."

"No...no, it's just that, I am..."

The tip of her tongue held the word, unworthy and Nat knew it. Releasing her pinned arm he caught her face between his large hands. "You are more deserving, more worthy than any Cherub or Seraphim I know. It is with my honor that I have claimed you. You wear your scars like a warrior. I am proud of you, Izzy for all you have done. Beauty is in the eye of the beholder."

He captured her lips, sealing her refute to his claim. Nat took his time, willing her to relax into his hold. When she did give into the kiss, flames licked his lips. Izzy wasn't gentle with her want and that suited Nat fine. He allowed her to take over, allowed her to dominate the kiss, her lips grasping his own with a fever he thoroughly enjoyed. Her tongue plunged into his mouth, snaking down his throat, a tease of what his body longed to do to hers. Their breaths mingled, hot puffs of air drawing up to the heavens, outlined against the cool of the night. Her hand slid around his head and her small fingers played with the bristly hairs on his nape. Everything she did felt like heaven.

Urgency had his hands roughly roaming over her form. She didn't seem to mind. When one of her hands snaked down between their bodies to touch him, he was the one stilling her movement. Nat wanted all of her, but not here. Not with the stench of the alley their perfume but common sense became a frayed thread. Their kisses, hard plunders of want and pent up desire aroused him like never before. Exposing more of her flesh, he watched goose bumps form on her tender skin as the cool of the night teased them both. Nat wanted to yank off his shirt, press his slick skin to hers but that might be his undoing. The restriction of clothing a tangible barrier he both hated and loved.

Nat reclaimed her lips, needing to kiss her senseless. She fought not to let her control break, not here, not now, and part of Nathanael understood her needing to remain in control. Nat liked this part of Isabella—wild and reckless.

"I need..." she croaked, her voice a sweet wanting balm urging him on when doubt dared to flare between their heat.

He nipped her neck, to mark her. She groaned from the sensation. "Tell me what you need, my *b'iā*."

"I cannot. The ache of what I want...I shouldn't...I can't."

She would and she can but Nat knew Izzy was warrior-built. She was not about to truly confess how much passion she craved and tonight he could only press her so far.

He played her to get what he wanted but part of it wasn't fair. He wanted her to want him for who he was not what he was born to and that realization robbed him of breath.

"My *b'iā* I want you, but not here. Not like this."

He silenced her with a hard kiss, knowing her body and his still sought relief. Tenderly he lowered her back to the filthy pavement, noting from the passing car lights her flushed face.

"Damn you," she spat.

"That you have my *b'iā*. That you have," chuckled Nat.

A resounding clap knifed through the air around them, instantly sending Nathanael's senses into a tailspin.

"Thought you'd never finish, Seraphim."

The deep voice slithered along Nathanael's skin. He didn't need to turn around to know a demon stood in the alley with them. Nor did he want to expose Isabella. Tucking Izzy to him, he willed her to remain quiet.

"Let go of me," she commanded, while buttoning up her shirt.

"Yes, do let her go, Seraphim. She has an urgent errand to attend to for me and it does not please me that you delayed her with your lust, which might as well have been a beacon for all my demons. Didn't know angel lust could be so colorful. Good thing I stuck around to ensure your safety."

The cold of the night did not penetrate Nat's heart like the demon's words.

Chapter Thirteen

IZZY CLUTCHED NAT'S dress coat tighter around her. She ignored all her sisters, who cast worried glances her way, to bee-line it to her bedroom. She longed to hop in the shower but that had to wait for another time. She'd put off facing Nathanael, not liking how he'd looked at her after what had transpired between them in the alley. They walked home in awkward silence. She hadn't cast one glance his way, even though the longing to see him ate away at her. Conflicting emotions surged through her. Izzy felt shame, she'd allowed her passion to take hold of her which made her realize she'd never shake her Cherub heritage.

"You let that demon live." His voice, rough with barely suppressed anger, ticked her off.

It was on the tip of Izzy's tongue to say, so did you. She barely nodded. "I need a few minutes of privacy." She didn't wait for his approval. Instead she yanked out a new shirt and a pair of skinny jeans, new panties and a bra and then marched with her obvious bundle into the bathroom. Rinsing her face with hot water, she took a second to look at herself in the mirror. *I look the same, but inside everything has changed.*

Something special had bonded them and it would hold for eternity, no matter what. She wondered if he felt the same. *Highly doubtful.* The cold reality of how fast she'd let her control slip with Nathanael shocked her. Izzy liked to think she was beyond her Cherub teachings but a desperate part of her longed for even more fulfillment from him. Giving in to that tempting desire would cement their relationship even more and that couldn't happen because she had no intention of ever leaving her sisters.

That heavenly high she'd felt from his kisses, the intoxicating rush had been more than she'd hoped for. And they hadn't even consummated the act. *By the path of light if we do that I might erupt into flames.* A soft giggle escaped her, startling Izzy.

No one warned her the longing to be with him would leave her doubting her sanity or questioning her independence. Being with Nathanael felt natural and right. *Then again why would anyone warn her she'd feel like this.* Izzy wondered if it was another curse leveled at her by the Mistress.

The hot water on her face renewed her. Dressing quickly she strode out knowing she had to confront Nathanael. Not liking what she had to tell him, she squared her shoulders thinking, get it over with.

"Did that demon touch you?"

The question caught her off guard. Nathanael breeched the space separating them to grasp her by the shoulders. That one contact curled her toes. When she inhaled she smelt their heavenly musk, evidence to the passionate story that had almost unfolded.

"He did, didn't he? You let that demon, that spawn of Lucifer lay a hand on you."

Izzy pushed him off her. "It's not like you think."

"Really, then you tell me what I should think?"

"That was no ordinary demon."

"Do you honestly think I am an idiot? I know exactly who that was."

It was Izzy's turn to balk. "You do?"

"Yes, of course. For the past decade the Dark Angel has been trying to send spies through the Heavenly Gates."

"Oh," said Izzy, sitting down on the bed. "Guess I wouldn't know that because I've been stuck here. He told me his name was Ash."

Nat scoffed. "That isn't his real name. No demon tells their real name because to know a demons' real name is to hold power over them. What did he want, Isabella?"

Izzy tried to ignore how the sound of her name rolling off Nathanael's tongue made her feel. She wished he'd sit, but his nervous energy vibrated like a flaming candlewick through him. She wondered for a moment what Nathanael would look like if he had his wings. *Wait a sec, he'll get his wings back now because he claimed me.* The thought she'd been played and used for his purpose rushed into her, fueling her need to maintain distance between them.

"What did he want?" repeated Nat, standing directly in front of her.

Izzy closed her eyes and instantly the scene of what she had allowed to happen to her in the alley with him lashed her. She should hate herself but she couldn't.

Opening her eyes she said, "He showed me Lucifer's army. It's huge. I saw thousands and thousands of demons, more than enough to storm the Heavenly Gates. That's what Lucifer plans to do. He's been luring humans, transforming them until they are full-fledged demons. I have never seen such a large army."

Nat sat down, ran worried hands on his dirty jeans. "Why? Why would he show you?"

It was the question Izzy had asked herself a dozen times. Why warn her? "I told him I'd tell the Almighty but you know I can not. I'm the Forsaken One. Even the Mistress will not listen to my prayers."

"Before we tell anyone, we need to know why. I do not trust the Dark Angel. Maybe this is all a trick."

Izzy sighed. "It didn't look like a lie. And, Nat, he is the one who took Shea's innocence, citing the ends justify the means."

For a second Nat looked stunned. She too knew how that felt. When he did speak it pleased her.

"We will find out what trick he plays and then we will avenge her."

Izzy smiled. She wondered if he knew he'd said 'we' not 'him'. Nat took her hands in his, kneeling beside her, further surprising her.

"I will leave you now and purify my soul to speak with the Mistress. I will ask her to witness our joining to perform the sacred ceremony now. We will not wait for another decade."

"Waiting might be good," said Izzy, softly.

Nat shook his head. "I do not want to wait. You are my heavenly wife. I want our union more then ever."

His cheeks blushed and for a moment he looked young and innocent. That warmed Izzy's heart. Her mind told her there was so much more to their joining for him than her, so once again she worked on rectifying a wall around her Cherub heart that yearned for her to yield.

So you can get on the Seraphim Council. That was on the tip of Izzy's tongue but she refrained from saying what she truly thought.

His fingers gently stroked her cheek. "Do not worry. We were meant to be together as the Mistress decreed. It's what I want."

"But is it what I want?" Izzy hated the hurt look that flew across his face.

"I ask that you give us a chance, Izzy. We can make it work."

Izzy sighed. "Tell her what the demon said." She desperately wanted to change the topic.

"The truth of the words can only come from you, Isabella. We must wait for the Mistress to honor us with her presence."

"Nat, you have got to be kidding. She will not see me. I have prayed to her—"

"Let me speak to her first and then we will pray together for her. She must see us."

Izzy clamped her mouth shut. His blind faith unnerved her. At one time she possessed that. No more.

"This might take awhile but never fear I have left you. I will remain in prayer until I hear from her."

That could be for eternity. Izzy withdrew her hands. "Fine. Go. Do this your way." *I will do it mine.*

With reluctance Nat got up. That pleased Izzy's beating heart. Having him kneel in front of her like he wanted to worship her made her skin itch for the feel of him. She'd have to learn to dampen down that affect of their heavenly union.

"Wait for me," he commanded, striding out the door looking like a warrior.

Nathanael didn't bother, once again, to wait for her reply. Seraphim born and raised he could not change what he was. Too bad she had.

SHEA AWOKE IN A JOLT. The feeling of being watched crawled along her skin. She clutched the duvet tight and forced herself not to scream. She knew he, the demon who haunted her dreams and who unleashed a tide of pleasure the likes she didn't want to think about, was in her bedroom, her sanctuary. When he acknowledged her awareness, Shea sucked in her breath. With the one blessed healing candle casting it's yellow glow she noticed as he calmly moved toward her that his wings were a deep shade of purple almost black but not quite. In the alley they'd looked black like the night but now the iridescent shades shimmered when he moved.

"I am surprised you are not screaming."

That voice of his, slick, commanding and sounding so proud did lots of things to her she did not want to think about. Dared not to acknowledge. "Why are you here?"

He stood staring down at her. She noticed his red glowing eyes were replaced with irises so deep brown they reminded her of melting chocolate. Since landing on earth, Shea had developed a sweet tooth and dark chocolate had been her favorite. No more. She'd stick to white chocolate from now on.

"I had to see if you were okay."

His words, unexpected, caused her to snort. Shea knew the sound was unbecoming of a Cherub but that had been the last thing she'd expected. "Okay? I'm great. Can't you tell?"

He smiled. Shea had been correct. His two dimples, boyishly charming, did not belong on a demon face. His skin, a tanned brown, easily made him look Greek. The wild wavy charcoal colored hair that reached his shoulders did belong to a demon for no angel had hair as exotic as his. It dawned on Shea then she didn't know his name and she wanted to. On the tip of her tongue to ask him, he further surprised her by folding his wings in and kneeling beside her on the floor of her bed.

A demon kneeling? Shea wondered if she dreamt this fantasy because it certainly started to feel surreal.

Speaking *scripture* the words flew out of his mouth. Shea cried at him. "What are you doing?" But she new exactly what he was doing even though it should be impossible. How? How could a demon know the ancient words of bonding to tie two souls together? *Why would he do this to me? How could he be the other half of my soul? Do demons even have souls?* Tears freely fell unchecked. Her entire body shivered.

His dark hand reached out and tenderly a finger wiped away a tear. Tenderness coming from a demon did not make sense. But she had experienced that and so much more in his arms. None of which she could confess to for none of what had happened to her made sense.

"Why?" she crocked, flinching from his caress. Heat blossomed inside of her and her eyes widened with the shock of how delicious his touch had felt on her skin.

"I find myself citing the ends justify the means over and over again in my head yet in this case I feel...I feel that they are hollow. I watched you try to cut yourself."

Shea shivered, clutching the duvet tighter while attempting to move further out of his reach.

"At first I did not believe what I saw. Why would a Cherub attempt suicide? You do realize that if you had succeeded you'd end up for eternity a slave to my father's realm.

Worrying her bottom lip, Shea wanted him to stop talking. His voice had a strange affect on her body. *Maybe I've got a fever.*

"Is that what you sought?"

"I sought to keep my honor," she spat, feeling the surge of anger roll past the arousal of his voice.

"It is as I thought. Well, my Cherub, you're honor has been avenged. I have claimed you."

"You can not claim me. You are demon and I am angel."

"Do you honestly think we are that different? And tell me, you did not feel the power of the words. I dare you." He chuckled at her.

The nerve of him. Shea felt like he mocked her and that further sparked her anger because she *had* felt the power of the words. She flushed. "The Mistress is the only one who can appoint my mate. This might be a concept you do not understand but you can't just claim me, it's a preordained thing."

He scooted to sit on the bed beside her, ignoring her angry glower. Shea scurried to the other side of the bed to place desperate space between them. A hand snaked out so fast, drawing her covered form to his that it wasn't until he loomed over her, when the scent of him, a delicious mix of heat and wild spices slammed into her that she realized the true taste of fear. It must have shown through her eyes, because his hold loosened and he allowed her more space beneath him. Still, his large body, full of bunched muscles unnerved her. A thousand miles would be to close, she thought darkly.

"My beautiful *fa'minua,* what if I told you your lovely Mistress came to me?"

"You lie," said Shea, trying to talk her heart into slowing down. "And do not call me that word."

"What word? Beautiful?"

A dark eyebrow perked up as he looked at her. Shea wished he'd look elsewhere. A simmering liquid of heat bubbled deep inside of her making her feel something she did not want to feel for this man. *Correction he's not a man, or an angel. He's a demon.*

"Get off me," said Shea.

"Not until you tell me what word?"

By the holy path of light is he flirting with me? Shea rolled her eyes.

He laughed. "The word?"

"Fine. *Fa'minua.* I'm not."

He moved up further on his arms, bracing his weight on his palms while looming over her. The look he gave her sucked all the breath from her and caused her insides to flutter in nervous anticipation. Pure male possessiveness stared back at her, banked by deep passion. His head lowered in a slow tease. Shea tried to look anywhere other than at his lips. She lost the battle. She noticed his eyelashes, so long they should belong to a girl, but on him they made him tempting. His strong nose and square jaw with refined cheek bones belonged on a classical angel face, not a demon.

"It has been a long time since I've spoken angel speak but I am sure I still remember my teaching. You're voice is *fa'minua*—the purest of heavenly sounds. You are the golden note. Correction, you are my golden note."

"I felt nothing when you said the words," snapped Shea, pleading with her eyes for him to get off her. He ignored her. His lips lowered until his warm breath teased her moistened mouth. Shea stilled, hating she recalled exactly how they had felt on her.

His tongue licked her lower lip, his leg shifted over her forcing her to open her legs under the covers to accommodate him. Glad for the thick duvet, Shea clamped her mouth shut.

"I did not think a Cherub capable of lying." He tisked at her, but kept using his tongue like a skillful sword. Wickedly delicious, Shea hated how much she liked the feel of his wet tongue as he licked at her lower lip like her clenched mouth did not hinder him.

"I..."

Should have seen that coming. The minute she opened her mouth, his tongue snaked in, his lips melded with hers and a volcano of desire, the same type she'd experience in that damn alley rose up sharply through her. Expertly he worked her mouth. A hand roamed until it stroked her hair. Everything he did, as before, tender and gentle—not at all what she had expected before or now. She sensed he held himself in check. His lips moved from her swollen mouth to her neck, pushing down the cover of the duvet until all of her neck was exposed. He mumbled dark words in a language she did not understand but her body did. When his hands reached up to frame her face the flicker of red embers glowed in his eyes.

"Do not think to ever lie to me again, Shea. I do not like it. You are mine. I have claimed you. Your honor has been saved. Do not ever attempt to take your life again. Trust me I will hunt you down in my father's realm and you will not like that. Trust me?"

"You've got be kidding? Trust you. I don't even know your name. And I can't trust a—"

"Demon," he added, looking mighty pleased with himself.

"Yes, I can't trust the demon who raped me."

"Is that what I did? I took something from you that you did not want me to have? Keep telling that lie to yourself but you have been warned. Do not lie to me again."

Shea sputtered. "I...

A loud knock startled them both. Attempting to push him off, true fear and alarm filtered through her.

"You have to leave," she panted.

He shook his head. "I am not leaving you until you admit the truth of what happened between us. You should feel no shame."

Hissing, she continued to push at his bulk. "I can not tell them I willingly allowed my virginity to be taken by you. You're nuts."

He cut her a smile. "That's exactly what I said to your Mistress when she sought me. See we are more alike than you thought." He eased off her, but his hands continued to caress her hair.

"Shea, can I come in?"

Isabella's voice felt like cold water on Shea. Of all the sisters she most did not want to see it was Isabella.

"Should I tell her to leave?" teased the demon.

"Stop touching me. I can't think," she whispered, pushing him off her.

He gave a satisfied chuckle.

"Shea, is there someone in there with you?" asked Isabella.

"You can tell her. She knows about me," admitted the demon.

Shea wildly shook her head. She hated having to refer to him as a demon. "What's your name?"

"If you willingly agree to be my mate I will tell you my true name. And, Shea, I should warn you that when we joined I learned all about you. I will look after you and your own. But I do not tell you my name lightly. I might be free of my father's realm but I am still demon. Knowing my name holds power. This I grant to thee my *b'iā* ."

Shea sucked in her breath. "What? What are you talking about?"

"I will tell you my true name. The rest call me Ash, but for you, only the truth. I know the secret you pray and sing to every day. I know..."

"You know nothing about me."

He glared at her. "I know you are twin born and that you pray for the safety of your sister. Cherubs can not share a soul but you do. I know you suffered like me in childhood to protect her. I will protect her."

"Leave her alone."

Isabella knocked louder. "I'm giving you two minutes Shea and then I'm coming in. We have something serious to talk about."

Noting can be as serious as this, thought Shea, looking desperately for a way to get him to leave without calling attention to Isabella.

His eyes lowered, the red banking to dark brown. "Trust is earned."

Shea stilled when he leaned over her. His mouth dropped to her ear and then the ancient scripture of his words—his name—trailed into her mind and body. It was the most beautiful, powerful word she'd ever absorbed. He backed off, nodded at her and then with one look of longing snapped his fingers. He vanished before her eyes, startling her. If ever she had to recall he was demon-born that was proof positive. No angel had power like that.

With shaky legs, Shea stood, moved to the door and opened it.

Izzy's eyes darted around the bedroom. "Who were you speaking with?"

"No one," mumbled Shea moving back to the safety of her bed. *Only the demon who has claimed me as his heavenly-demon wife.* Choking on that thought, she closed her eyes, her mind savoring the feel of his true name as it licked at her consciousness. He'd told her there was power in knowing his true name. She pondered what to do with it.

Chapter Fourteen

NAT AVOIDED THE SERAPHIM safe house. He couldn't pray or concentrate in the immaculate house filled with a gazillion electronic gadgets. His feet lead him to the place his soul sought relief and without fully being aware of it he once again stood on the steps of the Synagogue. Pushing slightly on the door, the openness of the Synagogue continued to surprise him. He stepped through the wide oak doors to be greeted by the Rabbi.

"Ah, it is good to see you again, my son. I would ask how goes your problem with your fiancée but by the look on your face things are not great. Am I correct?"

"It's complicated."

"They usually are," answered the Rabbi, ushering Nat inside with a smile and warm pat on the back.

Small talk had never been Nat's strong suit so he launched into what he needed.

"You are asking for me to lock you in a room with no food or water and not to worry." The Rabbi paused. Nat knew he wasn't done. "You test me. This is some joke, right?"

Nathanael stood his ground and shook his head. "Sadly no. I need privacy. Uninterrupted. If after seven days I do not emerge, I grant you permission to enter."

"Enter and find what? You dead on my floor? That's just what I need to deal with," taunted the Rabbi, looking clearly worried.

Nat wasn't immune to serving penance having recently completed a week of diligence. His sore back a reminder of the daunting task he set upon. *What choice do I have?* "Fear naught, I have suffered far longer. A week for me is nothing."

The Rabbi struggled to find the proper words but none came.

"There you go with that funny talk again," said the Rabbi, attempting to lighten the mood. Nathanael could tell when the Rabbi looked at him he saw something more than his human façade. "My son, your faith is strong. Let it guide you. Come, I will show you to a special room. It is not much, but you will have all the privacy you seek. But hear me, I will come charging in like a bull if I have not heard from you on the seventh day, make no mistake."

Nat chuckled. *This human does the good of mankind. Maybe they are not all that bad.* Nat was reminded how transformed his Seraphim thinking had become in such a short span of time on earth. *No wonder Isabella acts the way she does. Assimilating means change and in our heavenly realm most change equates a negative reaction.*

"Here, take this key. The door sticks so you might have to give it a good kick. I'm not walking down those steps. Body's not as young as yours. Now can I get you anything?"

"No. Thank you. I am honored by your kindness." Nat bowed, feeling as if he faced a Seraphim elder.

The Rabbi touched his shoulder. "I am not sure where you come from and for now think it best I do not know. I trust you. There is something pure in you and I shall take comfort in that. I shall leave you now. Lock the door behind you." He winked. "I have a spare key."

With that the Rabbi squeezed his shoulder, turned and left. Making his way down the sharp-angled steps, Nat used the key and then proceeded to kick the door open. Inside he made sure to lock himself in. He eyed the cold concrete floor and grimaced. Removing from his jacket pocket he took out the purple spiritual candle Meredith had handed to him on his way out of Isabella's building. He blew on the candle. His angel breath instantly caused it to flame. Placing the candle in the middle of the floor he disrobed, setting his mind to his task. Shivering instantly as the damp basement seeped into his bones, Nathanael prayed for guidance. Prostrating himself, he settled his bones in for a long wait.

"I WAS TALKING TO MYSELF," said Shea to Izzy.

Izzy didn't buy it. But she didn't want to upset Shea when she sought to comfort her. "I told Meredith a sister was to be with you at all times."

Shea scoffed. Calmly she slipped on a pair of jeans and a baggie hoodie. "Really, Izzy I am fine. I do not require a babysitter. You worry for no reason."

Izzy let the silence thicken the air, her eyes not once leaving Shea. "Great. Then you will honor swear to me you will not attempt to end your life."

She smiled, "I honor swear I won't."

That was too easy. Izzy's eyes narrowed as she looked at the Cherub. Shea seemed so tiny compared to the rest of them, but she always had been so. Tiny in height and small in frame, Shea had the most powerful heavenly Cherub voice Izzy had heard. She stood exactly five feet and was the smallest Cherub on record. A distinction she didn't like. That had been part of the reason Shea had been eager to take up arms with the rest of them. She wanted to prove her own worth. Izzy understood her motivation.

"Did they already eat?"

"What?" asked Izzy.

"I am hungry. Did my other sisters eat?"

Izzy smiled, feeling a bit like the fool. "Shea let us go together to find some food. I heard Nayla made one of her Mexican experiments again and I'm sure it will be delicious." Izzy still wasn't buying Shea's quick escape but the thought of eating one of Nayla's salivating concoctions was irresistible. Izzy's stomach grumbled. She wondered why they weren't all fat. Nayla had taken on the role as chef and none had dissuaded her. She worked daily miracles in the small kitchen

IZZY GREW ANXIOUS WITH the onslaught of each day and night. Time was her new enemy. Four days had passed since Nathanael left. She tried hard not to picture him lying naked in prayer, failing miserably. Izzy also didn't like worrying about his welfare. As stubborn as her, he'd starve in his quest to reach the Mistress, before giving in.

For the first time in a long while, Izzy did not know what to do. Always she took command. She'd been the one to find all her exiled sisters. The one to work her voice to ensure they had food and a roof over their heads. The one who used her smarts to save money, allow Michael to become her business partner while securing a building to house all of them. She sought to create harmony, to shelter them as much as she could from the wicked lure of the sins of man. Not always successful, it had still fallen to her. Now, since Nathanael had landed on their turf things had changed. Izzy realized she had slowly slipped back to the Cherub tradition that said let the Seraphim lead the way.

Sighing heavily, she decided she'd had enough of that. Taking a spiritual candle she lit it. Disrobing fast she pulled on a light white robe and cast the light from the blessed candle over her. Feeling purified, she went to her knees, stretched out her arms above her head and began to hum. Only when she'd centered herself, her breathing deep and even did she launch into a heavenly chant, opening her soul, praying for the first time for forgiveness.

"Isabella, thou may rise."

At first Izzy wasn't sure she'd heard true. When she turned her head and saw the Mistress' form hovering, fully cloaked, looking like she had ten years ago, Izzy was stunned.

"Thou may rise, my daughter. I am pleased by what I see in your heart."

Izzy did as instructed. The Mistress moved over toward Izzy's bed and then proceeded to sit on it. A number of reactions sailed through Izzy—dismay, surprise and a speck of fear.

"Thy time has been served well and now we have much to discuss," ordered the Mistress.

Turning to face the Mistress, Izzy made sure to keep her head bowed and her hands folded in prayer. "I am yours to do with." Speaking *in angle speak,* reciting the proper etiquette of words felt wrong to Izzy. She did it anyway.

The Mistress took Izzy's folded hands in her gloved ones. An electrical jolt traveled through Izzy. "It pleases me greatly you have not forgotten your Cherub traditions, my daughter."

Izzy tried not to grimace. She felt no more the Mistress' daughter than an angel.

"Tell me, how fare my Cherubs these last ten years in exile."

Izzy's head instantly snapped up to look up. "You knew?" Izzy blurted out the question without thought.

"Do not disappoint me with insular questions. I know all. Heed that," she admonished.

Izzy instantly bowed her head. "Of course, Mistress. I meant no disrespect. We have survived." Not much else did Izzy wish to disclose. *What was the point, if she's omniscient and all?*

"I had no doubt you would. Now about your Seraphim. The call is yours. Should I heed his prayer or do you wish to make him suffer more?" asked the Mistress, patting the spot next to her on the bed, inviting Izzy to sit.

So much for keeping with tradition. Normally during an audience with the Mistress the Cherub always knelt to show respect. Izzy slowly moved to sit down next to her, feeling awkward. "I am honored you think me wise enough to answer for Nathanael."

"He keeps to the decorum of his faith and expects a lot of you, Isabella. As he should. You are Cherub born."

Am I still? Wisely, Izzy banked that thought. She nodded. "He seeks to deliver a message to you for the Almighty."

The Mistress rose in one fluid movement from the bed to hover once again in front of Izzy. "I believe you are the messenger in this case. What else does your Seraphim seek?"

Part of Izzy didn't want to admit what he wanted, but it felt like the Mistress saw into her heart and head. Izzy looked deeply at the Mistress, trying to see a hint of eyes behind the black meshed veil that covered her face. The color and fine netting of the veil made that impossible. Taking a deep breath she answered. "He seeks your permission for the *b'iā* ceremony."

"Interesting. I had wondered if he'd be *Sera* enough to push his demands. I take it he has?

Izzy knew the Mistress knew he had been. A crimson blush stole over her features.

"My daughter, I am most pleased he has. He is your soul-mate. You are the heavenly host. Your charge of existence solely to usher in the next generation."

Izzy fought not to roll her eyes. *By the path of the holy light I am not ready for that.* "I beg thee, Mistress, find him another." Izzy rushed the words out fearful she'd let them go unsaid.

"What?" A gasp-like sound escaped the Mistress making Izzy tremble. "He displeases you?"

"No," said Izzy.

"He does not desire you?"

A vivid picture of what they had done days ago, their passion erasing common sense that said wrong time and place flashed hotly through her. "No," said Izzy softly.

"Then you are perfectly matched. Come, this topic is over. I would have you show me what the Dark Angel's son delivered unto you."

Holy mother of light she does not know everything. Immediately, Izzy tried to make her mind blank.

"My child, if I knew all, I would not ask for you to show me. Come, give me your hand. I warn you now hand-to-hand contact, flesh to my flesh, will hurt. This I must ask of you, my daughter."

It wasn't a question and Izzy knew it wasn't in her to refuse. *Okay, thanks for that warning. I think.* With awe, Izzy watched her remove a black glove. Expecting flesh, a golden glow outlined like a hand startled her.

"Come, my daughter. You must willingly touch my flesh. The pain will be much but you have not disappointed me."

That more than anything marshaled Izzy's thought. She smiled, feeling her heart sore with the Mistress' words. *I did not disappoint her.* She thought back to what had happened to her. *My wings were cruelly hacked off. There are protruding bones in my back that are constant reminders I've been mutilated, but I did not displease the Mistress.* Somehow that made her feel better and Izzy didn't like that. The injustice she felt for what had happened to her and her fellow Cherubs had been something she'd latched onto for years. Izzy wasn't ready to let it go.

NATHANAEL FELT HIS lids grow heavy. He knew he'd dozed off and on for the past days. In the dark of the basement he'd lost count of the days but praying for a visit from the Mistress was not for the faint of heart. A knock on the door interrupted his litany of prayers that automatically flew from his mouth.

A second knock swiftly followed.

"Nathanael you may come out."

Nat thought he must be hallucinating. That voice sounded like it belonged to Isabella. Impossible.

"Nathanael, do come to the door. Unlock it, now."

That sounded like his Isabella. He groaned in pain when he complied. Stiffly he got to his feet and with shaky hands managed to yank on his clothes. His head dizzy from the lack of food and water, he willed his queasy stomach to stop churning and grumbling. A losing battle. Using the key he unlocked the door.

"What are you doing here?" His voice cracked. She smiled. His heart flew to the heavens.

She pushed a glass of water to his mouth. "I've come to take you home."

Nat's eyebrows quirked as he downed the blessed liquid.

A piece of fresh bread that still felt warm fell into his hand.

"Eat it. And no, I mean back to my place," she clarified, grasping him under the arms to help steady him when he attempted to take a step out of the room.

"Here, I've got you. Do you think you're able to walk on your own or do you need me to get a stretcher?"

Isabella goaded him on purpose urging the *Sera* he longed to be to will the weakness away. "The Mistress did not come yet."

She tisked at him "That's okay. She paid me a visit."

"She paid you a visit?" Nat knew he sounded like an idiot but he must have heard her wrong.

"It took me getting on my knees and praying to her but yes, she did visit and she knows about the message and..."

Isabella's cheeks turned pink and she looked down at the concrete floor.

"And what, Isabella?"

Mustering her courage she looked him in the eye. "She knows about us and she's willing to complete the ceremony."

"Why do I get the feeling this does not make you happy?" asked Nathanael slowly chewing the piece of bread that tasted like heaven to his starved body.

"I am afraid, Nathanael, it will not be to your liking."

"It...you mean you. Trust me I think you're perfect."

"I am not perfect and well you know that. The Mistress has stated her demands," said Isabella helping him move up the angled stairs.

"And what are they, Isabella."

"She will perform the ceremony only if you are willing to stay with us."

The ramifications of what Isabella said took a full minute to be absorbed by Nathanael. "Are you saying she will not allow you back into the heavenly realm?"

"I think it best if she explains things to you, Nathanael. Trust me this is something we will need to talk about. Things are never easy when dealing with the Mistress. That I have learned the hard way."

Nathanael laughed, his vocal chords still sounded rusty. "Good to know we both agree on that. Before I dare present myself to her I need to eat and drink and take a bath. Are you willing to take me to your house now, Isabella?"

It gave Nathanael deep satisfaction watching Isabella gulp. She wasn't comfortable with him still, but he knew she wanted him to come home with her. "By the way how did you find me?"

Isabella's blue eyes looked at him. "The Mistress told me where you were."

Of course she did. She's probably been laughing her head off for the past four days while I've been dying of thirst, my body almost freezing to death. Nat didn't say any of what he thought. Nodding, Isabella escorted him from the building into the dark of the night. He wondered if his body could withstand the five block hike back to her building. He highly suspected Isabella did not venture into human vehicles. The compacted space, roar of the engine and stench of the vehicle's interior he'd gotten into only once had made Nathanael think only a demon could design something so hellish. Tonight, his strength further tested, he fought to put one foot in front of another, wishing with all his might he had his heavenly wings for support.

"Lean on me, let me help you." Isabella's heavenly voice poured through him. She offered her strength and the power of her voice eased his aching bones and muscles. When he leaned onto her, allowing her to take more of his weight, that unique Cherub fragrance of hers nailed his body with longing.

Who needs wings when your soul-mate is by your side? Nat didn't dare speak those loving words to Isabella. Still tough as nails when she was all Cherub, he'd save those endearments for later, when his body was back to full strength and brought them both the pleasure they deserved.

Chapter Fifteen

ASH WATCHED THE HUMAN climb the rail leading up to the Cherub's dwelling. What was he doing? Ash certainly didn't know what he was doing. He'd claimed a Cherub—one he'd only meant to absorb power from. Something he couldn't describe and didn't want to examine too closely had instead sailed through him from the moment he'd come face to face with Shea. His father would have a field day with that, probably roast a dozen slaves just to piss off Ash. Really, though this was all the Mistress' fault. Her taunting words or redemption had teased him to extremes. God I hate her. Now, he understood his father's wrath for her. Elusive, mysterious and powerful enough to rule if she so desired, she was not to be dismissed. He'd tried that but her voice always stole into his consciousness, whispering words of warnings he couldn't ignore. Well he could, but then he'd be obeying his father and Ash had made it his primary role to never do that.

"Do you honestly think they will offer salvation to you...a mere human?"

Gareth stilled his breathing, his body tensed for an attack, but Ash had already invaded the young man's mind. In Iraq when Gareth's senses had screamed evil he'd listened, and Ash knew he longed to confront a demon. Ash, however, was not like the demons the human had seen in Iraq. In fact he was so far from the soul-sucking demons who'd taken this human's friends it was why he'd gone to his own extremes. Tonight with the bite of the late October wind cutting through the human's bulky Celtics sweater, sweat trickled down his back. Fear had a funny why of making human's sweat even when their body froze in shock.

"Who the hell's there?" barked Gareth, rising to his feet. This human was always ready for a fight. In fact, Ash knew he longed for it.

"It is not hell that you seek but hell might yet take you."

Gareth barked a dry laugh. "Buddy, you want to do psycho-babble, take that shit somewhere else."

Ash laughed causing Gareth to tremor, even though he tried hard not to show his fear. Ash's esteem for the male rose a notch but not enough to turn the course of his actions. This human would be used for his purposes because he was not about to let Shea suffer. Her power had changed him and while he hated worrying about her, he did need to ensure Isabella, the leader of this exiled group of Cherubs, did as asked.

"I see why they have taken you into their fold."

Gareth didn't acknowledge the remark. When Ash stepped fully into the light cast by the half-moon, Gareth also didn't speak. The miracle of wings, the alien-like mystery, no longer surprised him but Ash wasn't an angel and Gareth was about to discover the huge difference separating them.

"I take it you are an angel," stated Gareth, trying to sound bored.

"Of sorts, human. So it is salvation that draws you like a magnet to them." Ash moved closer to Gareth. "It is good you are ignorant of who I am and what I could do to you."

Gareth smirked. A vivid image of feeling the warm flesh from his buddies mutilated body on his skin assaulted him and this time it was Ash trying to appear unaffected. Reading this human wasn't easy, thought Ash.

"You humans are so limited in your perception of evil. The things I could do to you...you would beg me for the mercy of what had happened to you in that war."

Everything inside Gareth stilled and if Ash hadn't had his increased powers this human would have been able to block him. "You reading my mind?"

"Of course, human, but soon your worries shall cease."

Ash's hand clasped Gareth on the shoulder. Searing pain blinded both Ash and Gareth as the connection was made. Ash willed his essence to seep into Gareth's mouth to stream inside of him. The human fought the conversation, first by choking and then trying to vomit. Ash's will would win the day. Shea needed him. With that thought utmost in Ash's mind, he forced himself again onto the human.

"I do this because I care for her and they will not welcome me into their fold."

Through the clenching pain in Gareth's gut, which Ash too felt to the core of his being, Gareth crumpled into a fetal like heap, his body bucking and spamsing, against what Ash was forcing. There was nothing Gareth could do to fight against Ash's hold.

"There is no other way. I must become you for them to gain my trust. Forgive me." The more Ash stayed in the human realm the more he understood the exiled Cherub's angst. A day ago he would never have thought to ask for forgiveness. It certainly would have had him killed in his father's realm. Forgiveness, thinking of another beyond oneself, was the single most punishable crime one could commit in Lucifer's domain and one Ash never forgot. Until, he amended, he'd touched Shea. *For eternity she might truly doom me.*

MEREDITH KNEW SHE WAS anxious. She slipped the red robe over her head, belting the gold-colored rope around her middle. With one last look at her room she walked out and made her way to the common room where the blessed ceremony would take place.

"Everything is ready," said Nayla, bringing in a second tray of food to the room.

A feast to celebrate the *x'simcha* ceremony, the joining of Isabella and Nathanael. Not nearly as celebratory as in the heavenly realm,

Meredith did want it to be remembered properly. *Tonight we will make it special. The younger ones need to see this. They need to realize the significance of this act. I beg of you again, Mistress, honor us with your presence.*

"Is everything the way you remember?" asked Nayla, bringing Meredith's mind around to the task at hand. She quickly surveyed the common room, taking in the subtle but efficient changes to the space.

"Nayla, once again you shine like a rare beacon of light. Everything is perfect. You even remembered to create the *uq'mulat*—the heavenly cloud cake."

"It will not taste exactly like it would..."

Meredith drew the sister closer for a loving embrace. "You always work a miracle. Tonight you did not disappoint. I know it will taste heavenly divine."

Nayla bowed her head, hiding a rush of thankful tears. "Would you be so kind, Nayla to ask Shea to bring in the black candle. We only need one."

"Of course, Meredith," said Nayla, rushing off to complete her task.

Like most of the sisters, Nayla loved a task. In fact routine was still so ingrained in all of them, Meredith suspected to be idle would truly break their spirit. And, maybe that is why Izzy formed the band. Maybe she sensed giving us all a purpose, telling us to quite literally sing for our supper, is what we needed to survive in this realm. And, just maybe that is why Izzy needs to still fight the demons even though she will not let us take up arms with her.

Meredith recalled a fonder time when the simple pleasure of holding a heavy sword made her smile. Izzy sheltered them on earth. She feared letting them get hurt but Meredith realized now she should have pressed more to follow her in arms. Their bond of anguish had united them in their heavenly quest to take up arms but Izzy didn't view it as the same here and Meredith needed to change her thinking. The future Meredith was seeing was not for the faint of heart and all arms on earth and in the heavens would be needed to stop what she suspected had already been set in motion—a human-demon turned army ready to overthrow the heavenly gates.

Forcing her mind back to the present, Meredith prayed Shea was up to the feast. She appeared more like herself and in a way that worried Meredith. What had happened to her she couldn't even think about, but Shea, like Izzy, donned a mask. But Meredith had seen that mask slip and what she'd glimpsed had her questioning Shea. Something she didn't like at all. Shea smiled, and talked with them all like nothing had gone wrong when Meredith knew inside a part of her died. *Maybe this is her coping mechanism.*

Immediately, Meredith's mind went to Gareth. *Of all the times to wonder about him, now is not it.* He hadn't shown up last night. Highly unusual. Meredith feared for his health. The affects of his withdrawal were lessening but she liked to think, blindly, he had need of her.

When all her sisters joined her, including Shea holding the significant black candle, Meredith addressed them. "You have all done a blessed job. Tonight is a true celebration. Now we must await their presence."

"No need. I am here."

Izzy's voice didn't sound happy. Meredith wondered about that but before she could approach, Nathanael walked in. Dressed in a purple robe with a red sash draped across his chest he looked as unhappy as Izzy.

So much for making this night special.

Nervous, Nathanael tried to push the feeling away. He tried to reason this as fate, but a subtle poke kept returning to nudge him that none of this was supposed to happen for another ten years. *Too late for that.* He wondered if being on earth affected his reasoning. He was young to claim his mate but according to Isabella, the Mistress had agreed to their joining. He might have uttered the binding words to keep Isabella tied to him but with the Mistress' blessing he'd be able to join the Seraphim Warrior Council and become a full-fledged *Sera*.

Isabella approached him. Her complexion looked even paler and he delighted in how she fidgeted with her sash around her waist. *She's as nervous as a newly trained Pegasus.* The thought charged through him. He was Seraphim, his burden to alleviate and wash way her fears.

"I think we should wait."

Her words, said as low as possible, spoke volumes.

"Too late."

"Let me petition her again to find you another."

Nathanael grasped Isabella to him. "There is never another. You are mine." He fought the urge to flee. Everything he'd worked hard to achieve would be within reach once the Mistress blessed their union. Isabella would adapt to life in the heavenly realm again. He wasn't blind to the fact that she'd miss her sisters but her penance served allowed her to enter the Heavenly Gates. She had also been the one to deliver the dark angel's message to the Mistress, so that counted for something.

"Meredith you may lead the chant," ordered Nathanael. Dragging along a reluctant Isabella they moved to the front, knelt down with the other sisters and bowed their heads in prayer. Again, Nat fought to clear his mind, and purify his soul. Isabella's fragrant Cherub body so close to his made him recall the alley and how their passion had almost been his undoing. Inhaling deeply, he thought of a blank wall, anything to control the arousal of his body.

"Rise and stand before me Nathanael, First Born of the House of Raphael and Isabella, my Cherub daughter."

Nat felt Isabella rise. He kept his head bowed hoping Isabella followed proper decorum.

"Thou may look upon me now for this blessed joining honors traditions and pleases the Almighty."

Nathanael rose his head to look at the Mistress. Covered entirely in white, instead of her usual black, as Cherub custom, the veil covered even her eyes. Not one speck of flesh could be seen. Around her neck she wore seven separate necklaces, each with a round wooden circle. In his robe pocket, Nathanael held the eighth penance circle, which belonged to Isabella. He'd tried to give it to her when he'd first arrived but she had not accepted it. Tonight he prayed she did.

"Thou art granted union but Nathanael and Isabella before you agree to the blessed union you must willingly agree to the terms."

Terms? Nat, pretty certain this did not follow protocol, felt his stomach tighten in dread. He didn't dare dart a look at Isabella but felt more than saw her form go rigid.

"You honor us, Mistress." Nat kept his tone respectful, shoving aside the fear clawing at his insides.

"So be it."

A blinding golden light filled the space and when Nathanael blinked he knew he was back in the heavenly realm. The warm loving caress of the wind told him home was close by.

"Kneel *Sere* and hear thy terms of joining."

Not one ounce of warmth filled her voice. Nat immediately prostrated himself as instructed, bowed his head and prayed. Without doubt he knew whatever terms she offered tested his strength in faith. He swallowed, feeling parched and worried, of what might be offered to Isabella. *I am Seraphim, warrior-ready to face this test.* He kept chanting that mantra inside his head, even when the Mistress started listing the terms. His heart thundered to a cold stop when the harsh reality of her words penetrated his shivering body.

"I beg thee, Mistress, do not ask him," said Isabella. Tears slid unchecked down her cheeks. She didn't care.

"Thou overstep thy boundaries, Cherub. Careful how thou approaches."

Izzy lowered her head, and forced a calming breath. None of it worked. *Everything is about sacrifices.* The Mistress outlined her terms to Nathanael and Izzy knew his faith, like hers, was being tested. *When is it enough?* It was a dark thought and she immediately purged it from her mind.

Izzy sought another approach, careful in deed how she spoke. "He is Seraphim, a warrior of faith, needed in the upcoming battle."

"A Seraphim warrior he longs to be. As of yet he is not. The choice is his. Do you accept the terms?"

What choice do I have? Keeping her head bowed, Izzy swallowed the rush of tears and nodded.

"So it is witnessed by thee blessed path of light."

A flash as blindingly bright as what had brought her to the heavenly realm moved Isabella into another room. The sight broke her heart in two. Her soul, heavy, ached.

What faith tested a warrior like this?

You were tested and survived.

The Mistress words crashed through Izzy, a powerful reminder she had agreed to the terms.

In the exact position, Isabella had been, Nathanael, wearing the starchy white penance robe, lay on the *Septuagint Council* floor. His father loomed over him, his booted gladiator sandals looked exactly the same. He didn't look remotely upset at the task the Mistress appointed him. *How could he not be affected?*

When Raphael grasped his son's right wing and brought it up taunt, Izzy felt her entire body stiffen, a surge of bile rising up through her. She didn't dare look away. Through the haze of pain she felt Nathanael's eyes on her. Steel-colored eyes filled with warrior strength and determination. Unflinching, his eyes shuddered close the second the sharp sword of the *Kita* severed his wing. With swift movement, his father yanked up his son's second wing. A choked gasp over-powered Nathanael. Isabella fell to her knees, knowing the torment of birthing pain his body gripped to. He did not scream. His eyes steady, he opened them to stare straight at her. With precision, Raphael severed his son's second wing. Not a word spoken. He walked away, leaving his son to the hellish pain his body had no choice but to accept.

Isabella rushed forward, uncaring of the warning from the Mistress. She could not leave him alone, not when she knew first hand how much agony his body undertook.

"You should not have accepted the terms." Her tears fell to the hard, unforgiving Council floor.

He gasped again.

"Do not speak. I know the torment you are going through."

Nathanael attempted to crouch to his knees. Isabella immediately moved to him. He flinched from her touch.

"I am sorry, Nathanael. I truly am sorry. I begged the Mistress not to ask this of you. Why, why did you agree to the terms?"

Squatting, his body still racked with tremors, he looked at her. "I made this sacrifice willingly because I am honored to be your chosen one. I love you Isabella."

"And I you, Nathanael." The confession in the midst of his gripping pain felt somehow hollow. Slowly, Isabella moved within reach of him. When he painfully attempted to draw her close, it was Izzy who wrapped her arms tenderly, with caution, around him. She cradled his head to hers, offering the healing of her voice. The ancient healing chant eased his sore body and for that she offered thanks to the Mistress. When his gray eyes looked at her with gratitude she felt like her heart and soul saw him for the first time. *He is my chosen. There is no other. I am honored to be his.*

Another blinding light surrounded them. Izzy looked up. They were in the exact spot they had been when the blessing ceremony started. She looked at Nathanael, he looked at her, clearly surprised. She could tell by his stance his body wasn't in pain.

How can that be?

"The Almighty is pleased with your willing sacrifice, Nathanael. Isabella, you are Cherub born and warrior ready to the task thou hast been appointed to."

"But?" asked Nathanael.

"You passed the test Nathanael and are *Sera* now, a true Seraphim warrior angel."

The Mistress placed a white gloved hand on Nathanael's shoulder. A shudder went through his body and then miraculously his beautiful white wings unfurled from a slit at the back of his robe. Shock and awe filled his face.

When the Mistress moved to Isabella hope flared briefly in her.

"Heavenly wings thou hast earned, Isabella, but to take them you must willingly accept the terms."

Izzy expected that. "I am honored, Mistress you find me a mere Cherub worthy of wings but I will keep to thy terms as agreed."

"So it is to be."

The Mistress backed away. "Kneel."

Izzy dropped to her knees, feeling Nathanael do the same. The *scripture* words sailed through the room filling Isabella with love.

"Bring me the candle."

With her head bowed, Izzy wondered who had been appointed to approach the Mistress. Not daring to look up she forced her curiosity to heel.

"I bring forth light to signify thy darkness purged from your souls. Together thou walk the righteous path of the light. One thou art until dust do thy make. Celebrate your journey with hearts and soul pure. You have the Almighty's blessings."

When she ordered Isabella to stand and bow her head, Izzy expected her to place the necklace around her neck. Instead, Nathanael's arms rose to cover her head.

"The journey the Almighty has asked of you, Nathanael and Isabella, is not for the faint of heart. That thee willingly suffered, sacrificed, shows thee pure of strength. With this blessing I grant you each a *Kita* to help purge this realm of darkness. Work with mankind to show them the path of light. Lead the human-born angels, as was foretold."

A gasp from one of her sisters broke through Izzy's mind. *Foretold? What is she talking about?*

The Mistress leaned closer to Nathanael and Izzy.

"For the greater good thee were taught. A foretelling written at the beginning. Teach the human-born angels to be warriors and be our first line of defense against Lucifer's growing army. When the time comes for thy battle at the Heavenly Gates thou all wilt be welcomed home. So thou art blessed."

With those words, the Mistress left as quietly as she had arrived. Isabella hadn't realized she had been holding her breath until Nathanael drew her into an embrace. When his lips claimed hers, inside she cried a mix of fear and joy.

Chapter Sixteen

ASH COULDN'T BELIEVE his eyes. He'd successfully taken hold of Gareth's mind, but still the human fought him. Crouched by the side of the recreational center he could easy see what was taking place inside the room. A joining between a Cherub and Seraphim. They didn't have time for this. The army his father was ready to unleash was almost ready. Did the Mistress not understand the urgency of his message? Surely not. He'd been quite detailed in what he'd conveyed to the Cherub. It felt like a blasted long time for the formal ceremony to end. When it was finally over, he noticed one Cherub in particular glancing out the window and for a second Ash wondered if she could see him. He almost laughed. No, that would be impossible. The power he'd amassed from Shea was a tangible pulse that continued to grow. And the only thing she'd spy if she did would be Gareth's human form, moving to lounge idly against the building. It was then Ash realized why Gareth struggled so much against his hold. He had feelings for this Cherub and did not wish her harmed. With a smile perfectly balanced on his lips, Ash made Gareth walk into the Cherub's dwelling. This Cherub would be the one to let the demon enter the sacred Cherub domain.

Meredith waited for the proper time to pass. Silently she eased her way out of the celebration. Turning down the hallway she spotted Gareth, leaning unsteadily against Shea's door.

"Are you all right? She advanced into his space. He didn't acknowledge her until she stood before him.

"Where is Shea?" His smoky-voice made Meredith take a step back.

"Gareth, tell me you did not give in?"

He turned, gave her a puzzled look and stepped away without answering. For a stunned second, Meredith did nothing. When she let the anger take hold of her, she marched after him and in a very un-Cherub-like way grabbed his sweater.

"It is not too late. You were doing good."

A hurtful scoff met her remark. "Good is over-rated. Where is Shea?"

Meredith felt confused. *Why is he asking about Shea?* She immediately reproached herself. He probably worried for her welfare. *I have no claim on Gareth. The reality is we can never be together.* Disclosing what she was had unburdened her soul but it had obviously been the wrong thing for Gareth to tackle.

"Shea is making her way to the recreational center for the celebration."

"Celebration?"

It was question but it barked like a command she rushed to answer. "The joining. Isabella and Nathanael have completed the *x'simcha* ceremony and the feast continues with a private party Michael has agreed to hold for us. Would you like to join us?"

"Is the Mistress here?"

"Yes." *How does he know about the Mistress?*

Gareth looked annoyed. His gaze shifted to the floor. "Great. That's just great."

Turning, he once again dismissed her to make his way back down the corridor toward the stairs. Meredith tried not to feel hurt and failed.

"Do you require me tonight to ease your pain?" She swallowed, feeling nervous for the first time in the human's presence. He stopped cold, pivoted and marched straight back to her. Something dark, feral and predatory awoke behind his flat green eyes.

"Ease my pain. That has a nice ring to it. Lead the way, Cherub."

"Why are you acting so strange, Gareth? And, please do not call me that name, again."

"What name?"

She snorted and rolled her eyes. "Cherub."

His eyes narrowed. "You do not like your name." He sounded slightly incredulous.

Meredith fought not to grimace. She'd told him exactly what she thought of Cherub tradition the night she'd shown him her wings. "It's not my name. It's a designation tattooed in invisible ink for all the other angels to see. I'm Meredith, not just a Cherub."

He applauded, the ringing sound of his mocking clap felt like he'd smacked her. "I'm not sure what has happened to you tonight but you are not the same."

"No, I am not, Meredith." His eyes softened as he moved into her space. "I am not mocking you. Your comeback took me by surprise. It seems there is much that continues to surprise me about you girls."

"I told you what happened to us."

"Yes, that is true, but I'd like for you to tell me again."

"What? Do you mean now?" She turned her head to look back the dark candle still flickering away in the common room and wondered if she'd be missed. The thought of watching Izzy and Nathanael act as a happy couple truly wasn't something she longed to witness. Then again, she probably should set an example for the others.

"Why are you hesitating with your offer? You thought to ease my pain and I find comfort in your voice. Lead the way."

Meredith looked again to see if any of her fellow sisters poked their heads out to see where she might have wandered to. *Guess they're all too caught up in the celebration to notice that I have left.* Selfishly she wished someone needed her. Gareth cleared his throat. He needs me, she thought, turning to face him with a practiced smile.

"I don't have a lot of time," she said.

"Then we had best use it wisely," he said, giving her a friendly wink.

He took her arm, something he had never done before. Meredith waited for the assault of his turbulent emotions. Nothing. A cocoon of blackness that did not overload her senses greeted her. Instantly, she relaxed, knowing something wasn't quite right but too happy to give him a second chance. After all everyone deserved another chance. She, more than him, understood the need for making a clean slate.

A TORNADO OF EMOTIONS churned inside Izzy. The need to confess rocked her. *What did I do?* The question, the only one haunting her for the past hours, damned her. She'd smiled, eaten the food at the feast and acted like all was normal even as Michael, her business partner, pretended to be happy for them all. He wasn't truly happy and she didn't need to be empathic to know the reason why. They had rocked the foundation of his beliefs and he still very much sought revenge. *How could it ever be the same? We are not the same.*

A gentle knock on her sanctuary door brought her upright from the bed. Nathanael, her husband awaited for her to open the door. This act, significant and symbolic, a part of Cherub tradition caused her stomach muscles to flutter madly. The meaning of what she was about to set in motion rattled like a wind chime blowing in the wind.

Izzy yanked open her bedroom door. He grinned, his eyes heated with warmth. They turned light gray, almost hazel-like when he was happy. Definitely asphalt-colored when angry.

"Get in here," she said, turning her back to march over to stand by the bed. She didn't dare sit on it. The act significant, and intimate, considering what she thought he hoped to do next. Izzy closed her eyes and wished again she'd changed into jeans and a shirt. Wearing the red robe felt constricting. Wearing nothing underneath it left her body vibrating anxiously. Knowing he wore nothing under his matching robe unsettled her more.

"Isabella, your loving welcome warms my heart."

He teased her. She wrung her fingers together trying to figure out how best to explain everything. "Nathanael," she began.

"Nat." He gave her a long, searching look. "Please call me Nat."

A repeat of an earlier conversation, she thought. A smile tugged at her lips. "Izzy, please call me Izzy. All my friends do."

One of his eyebrows rose. "Friends? We are much more than friends. Izzy, I should warn you that if you treat any of your human friends, or greet them wearing what I know is underneath your robe...I shall kill them."

He flirted with her. Izzy found herself tisking him. "Nat, we are angels. We do not go around killing people."

"My only defense is that I am Seraphim born and yes, I will kill any human who dares see you—"

Izzy laughed, cutting him off. "Nat, that is not going to happen. Come here, I need to explain something to you."

"If it's the birds and the bees, save it. We both know I know all about that. What I do promise you tonight is pleasure. Lots and lots of pleasure," he said, grinning in glee.

She took his hand in hers. "After what I have to tell you, you might not think that."

"Will what you tell me involve having my wings cut off again?"

She gave him a puzzled look. "What?"

He brought her hand up to his mouth, kissing her knuckles. The soft touch of his lips on her skin caused her entire body to burn inside and out. "My wings were clipped. Your wings were clipped. That is pain. I am sure I can handle what you have to tell me."

It took a lot of willpower for Izzy to remove her hand from his, but in the end she had no choice.

"I bargained the Mistress to let me stay here."

He gave a slow nod, his eyes searching her face.

"You have to understand I could not leave them. Because of me, my Cherub sisters are in exile. I will not leave them."

"I understand that, Izzy."

His tone quiet and patient caused her to gulp with dread. "No," she shook her head. "You don't understand. She offered me the heavenly realm and I refused."

"You did what you thought was right."

Agitated with his soft words, Izzy got up and began to pace the space in her bedroom. "You are not listening, Nat. I had nothing left to bargain so I bargained you."

He stood, stepping into her space, making her still. "Explain what you mean."

"I wasn't sure you'd go through with it, but I bargained that you would willingly give up your wings to be with me..."

His eyes clouded over and Izzy rushed the rest of what had to be said out. "I also bargained that you would stay with me in exile, on earth and not take a seat on the Seraphim Council."

His hands grasped her by the arms. "How did you know I would agree?"

"I didn't. I thought, I thought you'd leave me and then..."

"Then the Mistress would have no choice but to leave you too here, to this realm, which is what you wanted all along. You wouldn't complete your penance. How could you?"

"What would you have done? This is my burden. I will not leave them to the wild of mankind alone. I will not."

She watched him struggle. He let go of her, running his hands over the top of his head. She longed to feel the short bristly ends of his hair.

He looked at the bed and then back at her. Izzy felt her heart trip with fevered excitement and wonder. *Why is he not bolting for the door?*

"Are you sorry?" he asked.

For the first time Izzy willingly got to her knees before him. Bowing her head low she crossed her arms across her chest. Speaking angel speak, she said. "I am sorry for the pain I have caused you."

He reached down and gently scooped her up into his embrace. "I would have done the same. You are a warrior and leader for your Cherub sisters. I willingly admit I wish there had been a less painful way but I understand your motivation. And now it is my turn to apologize."

"What?" she asked.

"I claimed you when I knew you were not ready but my own fear that you would leave me forced my hand. I took your choice away..."

"I give it willingly."

"Yes and no. We both know that. But come, let us make amends tonight. This is a blessed night and I plan to worship and love all of you until dust do us make."

"How can you still claim to love me when I've forced you to give up the Seraphim Council seat? That's the only reason you came after me."

"It appears, Izzy, that Seraphim's can change."

"But what about your father?"

A guarded look briefly crossed his face. "We were never close to begin with. I'm not saying what he had to do was easy but that's his role. He didn't flinch when he severed your wings and he was as steady for me. I hope my training will help us with the new *Kitas* the Mistress gave us because we are going to have to be the ones to train your sisters. And, honestly I don't need to sit on the Seraphim Council when my heart knows the path we have both been set upon is so important. You and me, working together, something I would never have thought plausible a few short weeks ago but you, Izzy, you my b'iā, have changed me for the best.

Izzy hated the tears she could not control. His words, flattery, warmed her heart more than the blessed ceremony they'd just undertaken. Gently, Nat touched her cheeks, slowly wiping away each drop, tearing open her heart more with longing and that wouldn't do.

Looking up at him, she sighed. "You're going to hate me more."

"Never say that Izzy. I could never hate you. You are mine."

"What if I confessed that I'm not ready for all of this. I know I'm asking a lot of you, but I'd like us to go slow. Let's date."

One of Nat's eyebrows quirked up and damn if Izzy didn't like how cute it made him look.

"I take it this is another human thing," said Nat, not sounding as angry as Izzy feared.

Nodding, Izzy rambled on about what dating meant to humans and how it worked. "Let's get to know each other more and then when it's right we can...you know," she said, a blush staining her cheeks.

Nat scooped her up onto his lap. She clutched at the lapels of her robe causing him to grin.

"For you only, my b'iã I will do this. This journey we are embarking upon is not for the faint of heart and I know you are a brave warrior but I find the idea of this dating thing intriguing. Just how long do you think we will undertake this?"

Izzy snuggled closer to him. His scent, leather and cinnamon enveloped her senses and Isabella wondered if she'd have a harder time with just dating than him. Still though it was what she wanted. They might be married and bonded together but that didn't mean they knew each other. It didn't mean they should rush the knowing either. "I don't have a definite idea of time but let's try a year."

He laughed, hugging her tight. "Six months. We will do this your way and then I plan to kiss my demands all over your skin and there will be no saying no. Understood?"

Demanding as ever. Izzy hadn't expected him to acquiesce so easily so she simply smiled and nodded. In six months they could try round two of this discussion and see where things went.

Izzy gave into the urge to kiss his neck and loved how he shuddered. She did so very much like to tease him. "I have been thinking of the Mistress' words and the vision the Dark Angel gave me. We will need more than the nine of us. We need to recruit the earth-born angels."

Nathanael looked aghast. "Isabella you can not be serious. The Seraphim safe house is filled with earth-born Seraphim and trust me the only thing they can wield is a pen."

"I know. It is much the same for the earth-born Cherubs. They are more concerned with make-up, fashion and fast cars. And, stop grinning. This is serious stuff.

"How on this earth can I not grin? You have fought me the entire way but we are finally united."

"Men are all alike," sighed Izzy with a sexy smile. "Easily diverted from the task at hand."

His hand reached out to play with her hair. "Or easily swayed to attend to more important matters."

"Nathanael I am serious, we need more angel warriors if we hope to stop Lucifer's invading army."

"Meredith might be able to help us with that. She can see the future and—"

"What are you saying?" asked Izzy, her body going rigid.

He cupped her chin. "I thought you knew. She catches glimpses of the future. I read her mind when I first arrived and caught that. I had assumed she had told you."

"No she had not," said Izzy, clenching her teeth.

"I am sure she has her reasons," said Nat, moving to once again play with her hair. "After all I'm fairly certain you have not shared all your secrets with her."

Izzy titled her head so she could look Nat in the eyes. "Did you read my mind?" Izzy would kill him if he said yes.

His lips skimmed hers, a tease of a kiss when she wanted more. "Sadly, no. I tried but when it comes to you, Izzy, I get nothing. I think I know why."

"And that would be?" she urged, lightly nipping at his lips.

"Because you can't read the person you love with your mind, it has to come from the heart and soul."

Izzy thought his poetic prose the most angelic thing he'd ever spoken. Chasing his lips, she kissed him with a passion that took him by surprise and that pleased her even more. The last thing she wanted her Nathanael to know was all the tricks she had up her sleeve. Some Cherub secrets needed to remain.

Epilogue

ASH SAT IN THE CORNER of the common room safely disguised as the human Gareth. He'd been invited in because Gareth had military training and Isabella and her devoted Seraphim warrior, Nathanael wanted to use his skills to help train the earth-born angels. A shiver passed through Ash which surprised him. He hadn't known there were such things—earth-born angels who were anything but angelic. The men were pen pushers, more at ease in their business suits and iPhones and sadly the women weren't much better. Ash concentrated. Paying attention to what Isabella and Nathanael wanted to do was a momentous task but a necessity. However, these earth-born angels seemed powerless.

A movement at the door caught his attention. Turning he watched two late twenty-something men saunter in. Unlike their brethren they'd casual copped a seat but what made Ash smile was the fact they looked nothing like their brethren. They wore casual jeans and their six foot-four athletic physique made him smile. Two young women, both looking pissed to their core strode in behind them. These two women, Ash suspected were probably not quite twenty years of age, and what set them apart was neither had the wheat-blonde hair of their fellow model-looking earth-born angels. In fact, one had a nose ring. Ash made a move to offer his seat to the one with the stud in her nose but Izzy urged him to stay where he was. Since she controlled this meeting of angels and since he was quite literally dying to hear how she was going to marshal this rag-tag group of misfits into warriors he swallowed his protest. The minute the meeting was over he had to leave. Staying full-time in the body of Gareth was absorbing too much of his power and Ash needed that power if he was going to play a pivotal role in the upcoming battle. A battle his father planned to win at all costs.

An hour later the first meeting was over and much still had to be worked out. Michael, the manager of the recreational center had offered use of his place to hold weekly meeting but honestly he thanked the pits of hell when Izzy stressed weapons training was more important. The only earth-born angels who confessed to wielding weapons turned out to be the four late comers. Four more, three men and one woman, from the group of sixteen who'd come to the meeting said they'd be willing to learn but Ash suspected it would take more time to train them then they had.

Nathanael spoke up when the meeting was almost over. "What we need is a gym for training."

"Give me a day and I'll make a few calls. I know a few guys who own some places and they might be able to help."

"Yes, but can they help with discretion. We won't be training like ordinary humans."

"A day. Give me that," said Michael, causing both Nathanael and Izzy to nod.

Only once the meeting was over and everyone had left the room did Ash stand to move to the window.

"Did you enjoy yourself?"

He waited a heartbeat for the Mistress to answer. She'd been in the room the entire time and while others might not be able to sense her, the same could never be said for Ash.

She materialized next to him and as always Ash hated how awed, and how unangelic he felt in her presence.

"Why did you not come to me to relay your message?"

Ah, thought Ash, the true meaning of why she haunted him. What could he say? The only out for him from his father's ever watchful realm was by means she would not adhere to. Would that suffice? Probably not. Not bothering to look at her, for that always hurt, he answered tactfully, aware at all times her power was as unlimited as his dear old Dad's.

"You don't always heed my messages and I felt time was of the essence. I merely did what was necessary to justify the means."

"Is that what you tell yourself, son of Lucifer? It is a falsehood as well you know but thee have not offended. Thy guise you keep is unnecessary. Your skills would be better applied to the task at hand as thyself."

God he hated angel speak. The sound always grated his ears. "They are not ready for me. They think I've taken one of their own against her terms."

"Shea."

He nodded. The longing to say her name a tease he fought to ignore.

"She should set them straight."

That made Ash turn to face the Mistress. He wondered if she knew all the angst his beloved held tight to her heart and soul. The thought she might and had nothing to divulge was more like it. Heaven might be beautiful and blessed but he suspected it was a facade. That he knew first hand from his father's warnings. "Leave Shea to me."

The Mistress turned, giving him her full attention. The power that radiated from her covered form caused the hairs on his body to stand on end.

"Shea is your intended whether thee like it or not.

The thing with that statement was Ash liked it way too much and that was never a good thing.

"These earth-born angels could do with a demon training them. Think on this."

Ash had been doing that and wondered not for the first time if the Mistress was reading him. He prayed not.

She took a step back from him and then said, "As it was foretold it shall be," disappearing on the last word of her sentence.

Ash laughed thinking she was as dramatic as his father but he also thought, "For our sakes I hope you're wrong."

Ash knew first hand that a war was about to be unleashed on the Heavenly Gates and if those gates fell they would all be doomed.

stay tuned for
Redemption
Fallen Angels series, Book Two
By Renee Pace

Chapter One

SHEA CLUTCHED THE BLANKET tight to her shivering frame praying for solitude or a way to end the ache etched deep within her. She stood as straight as she could, hidden almost behind the long white curtain that concealed her bedroom window. With only the sliver of a moon shining through the cloud covered Boston harbor, her room was awash in grays shadows. The angle of her stance allowed her to easily observe the scenery of the night. And, night, not day had lately become her favorite time. A month ago that had not been the case. Sun streaming from the heavens made her smile. Now it beckoned her tears. She shivered but not from the ever feeling of cold but from the loss of what had been.

As usual, she found solace nestled in the shadows of her room. She had no reason to be cold. Her bedroom heat had been cranked up earlier but no heat penetrated her body these days. Well, that wasn't entirely true. Heat soaked through her cells when she least wanted or desired it and that alarmed her. Her gaze once again turned to the mirror by her dresser. As always her new look shocked her. Gone was the golden-hue color of her hair. Now it looked as if it had been bleached. Hair, now as white as angel wings, mocked her. Shea hated her hair.

When she first woke that morning two weeks ago and discovered her change, she'd mustered her courage and hacked off her long strands. It didn't matter. She was cursed. Her hair had of course grown back, long thick and eerily white—a stamp to all her Cherub sisters of what had befallen her. Her sisters had not said a word to her of it. To speak of her ill, her falling into disrepute, was not their way.

Willing a calm she never felt these days, Shea tried once again to reach out to her twin. As always the voice that had been her constant companion was empty. Tears ran unchecked down her cheeks and the willpower to wipe them away seemed useless. And, just like that, the heat of arms Shea didn't want to welcome, didn't want to acknowledge, slid around her with ease. Deliberately, and carefully, Shea fought not to move, not to lean a fraction back into his heated embrace, even though a part of her ached to do just that.

He didn't demand answers. He didn't ask questions and that was telling in itself. He knew what she ached for. He knew she was now loss to the world she had been born into and nothing could change her path. And all of it was because of him. It was always good for Shea to ground her thoughts with his wants, his demands and the curse of his consequences that had befallen her.

"I will make this right," he said.

His hot breath on the back of her neck, even though her long thick hair covered her flesh, sent a cascade of goose bumps rippling across her flesh. Shea told herself it wasn't desire, and even that self-inflicted lie left a sour feeling in her stomach.

His arms pulled her tighter to his muscled frame. But, Shea knew if she turned around he would be invisible. He liked to camouflage the night with his body but deep down Shea knew he didn't want her to see him as he truly was—demon. She'd cursed him enough the first few night he'd offered comfort and deep down Shea wondered if her words had wounded him. Heavenly doubtful. He's a demon. He used me to get what he wanted. He took from me my power and now because of him, I no longer hear my sister.

For a moment Shea thought of the irony of her life. She too had become a fallen angel and now thanks to Lucifer's son she was even more cursed. Who would have thought that possible? Certainly not Shea when she'd willingly taken up arms in Isabella's fight for Cherub independence. Of course, Shea's motivates were much more driven. She had thought independence would enable her to free her twin. But alas, that had been a foolish desire. The only thing she'd done was to cause more strife to her beloved sister. A sister, who not once had Shea had the privilege of seeing or dared to acknowledge. But from their first breathes they had shared a special bond. They were telepathically linked. Shea truly believed they even shared the same soul, but voicing such was blasphemy. One soul for one person and that is why angel twins didn't exit. Or so she'd been told since the beginning of her Cherub teachings. Lies. All of it, and Shea even at a young age, had known it best to keep her secret sealed.

"Trust me. I will make this right for you and her."

The confidence of his words should have been a warning to Shea but that alone feeling she'd been trying to hide from her fellow sisters was too much for her to bare. She had never been strong like Isabella or Meredith. She never had reason before.

Shea turned, his arms sliding slightly away to allow her to melt more into his embrace. "I want you to let me go."

"Never."

It was the same argument over and over they nightly played with each other. He, her invisible demon who only dared to darken her room when the night's shadows allowed him privacy, and her, the cursed fallen angel who felt more useless by the blessed prayer bells.

His lips when they found her mouth were soft and questing but Shea kept her distance. She didn't deserve to feel when the anxiety of what she had lost, of what she feared darken her mind more and more. What if her sister had died? What if his taking her power doomed her more?

Shea stiffened and he finally released his hold on her to allow her to take one step away. She knew he looked at her but the same could not be said of her.

"Show yourself."

He laughed, the sound dark, rich and lush. She liked it but bite her tongue before speaking such.

"Why? So you can curse my demon form again."

Shea found herself smiling. Her words had held power over him. She tucked that information deep inside. "I will stay my tongue. I have need to speak to you face to face."

The words no sooner said than his solid form materialized an inch from her. Shea couldn't help herself. As always his beauty took her breath away. Sinfully ironic. His eyes, the color of deep melted chocolate were direct and assessing. He took a step back, allowing her to inspect him further should she wish to do so. And, Shea did. That too she couldn't help. He wore dark jeans, a black shirt and a black leather jacket. His wavy charcoal colored hair teased the tips of his ears and was slightly longer than she recalled.

"Do I meet with your approval?" he asked, mockingly but Shea caught the hint of vulnerability.

"I am sorry I called you names."

"No, you are not. Do not lie to me Shea for I will taste your lies. There are no secrets between us."

My whole existence has been a secret. Stilling her thoughts, Shea gulped. "Will you help me?"

He lowered himself to his knees, the sight beguiling her senses. She wanted to tell him to get up off the hard wooden floor of her room but knew he wouldn't.

"You are my bia. My chosen one. I will do all within my power to make you happy."

The words she knew he'd say. The words she'd hoped and didn't dare pray for because what she was about to ask, she could ask no other.

Dropping to her knees so that for once they were both keenly aware of how well they matched each other, Shea spoke what needed to be said. "Save her."

She didn't need to say the rest. As always he knew. He bowed his head slightly. "For you anything. Thy will, will be done. I will return with the want of your heart but I demand something in exchange for this burden you have asked of me."

By the holy scribes, I did not anticipate that. Feeling like her throat was parched, Shea found her courage. "Haven't you taken from me enough?"

For a moment a look of anguish and regret flirted across his too-handsome proud face. A face that held power and her destiny and Shea wished for a second she had not bothered him with the desire of her heart.

"We are not having that discussion again for you and I will always disagree on the motive. You are asking me to risk life and limb, to venture in the Heavens, when you know I am demon-born. If they find me, I will be killed. What I demand is simple. You."

Shea did gasp this time. He couldn't possibly mean what I think he does? Biting her lips she tasted the coppery scent of her blood, liking it a little too much. "I need clarification for what you are asking of me?"

His right eyebrow rose slightly, almost like he approved of her testing the terms of their agreement.

"Do you? You know perfectly well what I am asking. I want a night with you. To be even more specific. A night in your bed with you. Is that too much to ask of my bia?"

Shea fought not to cringe. She hated that word. Hated how much power was behind such a simple three letter word. She was his bia, his pre-destined wife, and as much as she fought against it and would continue to fight against the bonds that drove them together she knew in her heart she'd cave to his demands. She'd do anything for her sister.

"Fine. Bring my sister to me and your demand will be met."

He chuckled again. "We are not so dissimilar, Shea. I will do as you have asked. In my absence think fondly of me."

Shea couldn't help herself. She snorted on her laugh. "Think fondly of you..."

It was on the tip of her tongue to say the word 'demon' and like he knew it, and he probably did, he simply smiled at her. By the blessed path of light no demon should look that good smiling. Shea wisely kept that thought to herself.

Being born into the heavens, sacrifice was the second lesson of learning. All Cherubs were taught from the moment they walked that will and sacrifice were part and parcel of the Almighty's paths. After all, a Cherub's whole existence was one of sacrificing for another. The Mistress chose the Seraphim to be their mate and love had nothing to do with the heavenly terms that bond them for eternity. While Shea didn't have a Seraphim warrior to cater too, it appeared by the blessing of the Mistress, she did have a demon. And, if that demon was willing to do what she knew no Seraphim would dare, then so be it.

She'd sacrifice everything and anything for her sister. Sacrifices were nothing new for Shea. Her whole life she'd learned to do without to help in some small way for her sister and if she had to bleed or give into the demon's demands she'd willingly do so. After all, her life mattered naught anymore.

other books by renee pace:
chosen by the sea, A Siren's Lure Series

EVERYONE WANTS TO BE normal. After a boating accident in the summer, nothing will ever be normal for Gemini again. Pulled under by a rogue wave, Gemini drowned. Beneath the surf she transformed into something...other...but she can't remember what.

Since her resurrection she's been haunted by the lure of the sea. The pills her mother forces her to take do nothing to keep the mystical world at bay. No one believes her, not her family or friends. In self-defense against the mocking high school crowd, Gemini dresses as an EMO. If she can't be normal then no one needs to be close to her. A heartthrob of a boy with powers she's afraid of says he's her protector, while the new boy in school, the Captain of the Hockey team, simply wants to be her boyfriend. She's not sure who to trust and things become complicated when her parents are kidnapped.

Outside of trying to pass math, Gemini must learn how to embrace the pain of transformation and return to the sea. All this while trying to learn exactly who and what she is. The power of the sea can't be denied.

NITTY GRITTY NOVELS
OFF LEASH

WHEN LIFE KNOCKS YOU flat on your back, and you know you've had enough, try telling that to a dog demanding his walk.

Jay Walker is a fake. He acts full when starved and happy when sad. How else is a guy who has a deadbeat for a mother and a sister battling cancer supposed to feel? And isn't walking a pet just a chore? Too bad the dog doesn't know that. The dog lives in the now, embraces life to the fullest and gives his whole heart when offering love.

Off Leash is unique because it showcases issues of poverty that transcend countries, age and color. Alternatively told between the POV of both Jay and the dog, Ollie, it shows the reader how a boy who wants a job to make some quick cash so he can buy food for his cancer-stricken sister struggles with trying to do the right thing in a world that has treated him wrong since birth.

OFF LIMITS

LINDSAY LOOKS AND ACTS like the perfect fifteen year-old, but she's hiding a dirty little secret that no amount of fashionista coverings can make better. Telling her mother her step-father is molesting her is not an option. Trying to kill herself again haunts her more than the scars on her wrists, and pretending to be perfect at school might very well drive her over the edge.

Megan knows all about lying. It's been part of her life ever since she realized the only way to escape her poverty-stricken neighborhood was to work hard, keep her mouth shut and wear a mask no one can penetrate. All that changes when Lindsay befriends her.

Can two girls who have little in common discover the value of a real friendship or will the secrets they dare not speak destroy them both?

OFF STROKE

THE HARD KNOCKS OF life keep piling up for Eje. Born into a country on the brink of civil war, he knows the real meaning of survival. After a decade living in Canada, things aren't getting any easier but if he can keep his head down for his last year of high school he thinks there might be an out for him from his poverty-stricken neighborhood. Too bad fate likes to throw fastballs at Eje and he's forced into an afterschool paddling program. The Aquatic club is filled with white kids, who like to run for fun and paddle for performance. Eje has talent but liking paddling doesn't mean much when you're another kid from the projects.

Shannon used to live to paddle. After a drunk driver crashed into the car holding her and her mother, life has been anything but normal. Re-learning how to kayak isn't fun, and trying to find out where she stands with her once BFF's at the club reinforces how much has changed. Before the accident she'd never give a newbie paddler the time of day, but the minute she meets Eje all that changes. Unlike the guys at the club Eje's mysterious without trying.

When ultimatums threaten to end the afterschool paddle program and secrets get revealed will Eje and Shannon forget their friendship for the good of others or trust each other to do right? Two teens with little in common tackle prejudice and stereotypes to risk it all to help each other.

Off Balance
Nitty Gritty Series, Novella

JENNIFER'S SECRET IS big but she loves Charlie enough to know ending their teenage relationship will set him free and enable him to join the Army. When Charlie discovers the truth it's up to him to convince Jen their young love was meant to be.

ABOUT RENEE PACE

RENEE PACE GREW UP next to the Atlantic Ocean in Nova Scotia, Canada. She writes realistic nitty gritty novels where teenagers come of age and edgy dark teen paranormal novels. When not writing, she's an active community volunteer. Pace is a member of Romance Writers of America, and Romance Writers of Atlantic Canada.

Her first nitty gritty novel, Off Leash was a semi-finalist in the 2011 Amazon Breakthrough Novel Contest and has been in the Top 100 Amazon Paid ranking for Best Coming of Age story numerous times.

Check out her books at www.reneepace.com.

She can be reached on Facebook at http://www.facebook.com/ReneePaceYABooks twitter@ReneePaceYA

Email: reneepaceauthor@gmail.com

Don't miss out!

Visit the website below and you can sign up to receive emails whenever Renee Pace publishes a new book. There's no charge and no obligation.

https://books2read.com/r/B-A-ZTM-IZQV

BOOKS 2 READ

Connecting independent readers to independent writers.

Did you love *Salvation*? Then you should read *Chosen by the Sea, Book One*[1] by Renee Pace!

[2]

Everyone wants to be normal. After a boating accident in the summer, nothing will ever be normal for Gemini again. Pulled under by a rogue wave, Gemini drowned. Beneath the surf she transformed into something...other...but she can't remember what. Since her resurrection she's been haunted by the lure of the sea.

The pills her mother forces her to take do nothing to keep the mystical world at bay. No one believes her; not her family or friends. In self-defence against the mocking high school crowd, Gemini dresses as an EMO. If she can't be normal then no one needs to be close to her.

---

1. https://books2read.com/u/bzlYGm

2. https://books2read.com/u/bzlYGm

A heartthrob of a boy with powers she's afraid of says he's her protector, while the new boy in school, the Captain of the Hockey team, simply wants to be her boyfriend. She's not sure who to trust and things become complicated when her parents are kidnapped.

Outside of trying to pass math, Gemini must learn how to embrace the pain of transformation and return to the sea. All this while trying to learn exactly who and what she is.

The power of the sea can't be denied.

Read more at www.reneepace.com.

About the Author

Renee Pace grew up next to the Atlantic Ocean in Nova Scotia, Canada. She writes realistic nitty gritty novels where teenagers come of age and edgy dark teen paranormal novels. When not writing, she's an active community volunteer. Pace is a member of Romance Writers of America, Romance Writers of Atlantic Canada. Her first nitty gritty novel, Off Leash was a semi-finalist in the 2011 Amazon Breakthrough Novel Contest and has been in the Top 100 Amazon Paid ranking for Best Coming of Age story numerous times. Check out her books at www.reneepace.com.

She can be reached on Facebook at:http://www.facebook.com/ReneePaceYABooks

Read more at www.reneepace.com.